"Do you think I'm feminine?"

What? When Ann looked in the mirror, didn't she see what he saw?

She didn't wait for his reply. "I can't cook. I don't know anything about kids. I can't sew. I—"

Dean stopped her rant. "You, Ann Billings, are the most beautiful woman I've ever seen."

For an instant, everything froze.

Then he was lost to the wonder of her smile.

Then it faded. "Sorry. I was having a pity party and I dragged you into it."

"You think I said that out of pity?" The woman was clueless! "You know, the only masculine thing about you is your stubborn inability to see what's in front of you."

"Huh?"

"I'm talking about me!" he snapped.

She looked stunned. "I didn't… I never…"

The words just died away, and that was all he could handle.

"I have to go." He stepped around her and kept on walking. Had he just revealed he'd carried a torch for her for years?

Oh, what had he done?

Arlene James has been publishing steadily for nearly four decades and is a charter member of RWA. She is married to an acclaimed artist, and together they have traveled extensively. After growing up in Oklahoma, Arlene lived thirty-four years in Texas and now abides in beautiful northwest Arkansas, near two of the world's three loveliest, smartest, most talented granddaughters. She is heavily involved in her family, church and community.

Her Single Dad Hero

Arlene James

HARLEQUIN® LOVE INSPIRED®

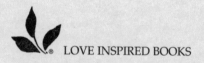 LOVE INSPIRED BOOKS

Recycling programs
for this product may
not exist in your area.

ISBN-13: 978-0-373-89916-6

Her Single Dad Hero

www.Harlequin.com

Printed in U.S.A.

Do not conform to the pattern of this world, but be transformed by the renewing of your mind. Then you will be able to test and approve what God's will is—His good, pleasing and perfect will.

—*Romans* 12:2

I know some truly intelligent, talented, loving, beautiful professional women, and quite a few of them live in Oklahoma, but only one is my niece. Hillary, your many accomplishments speak volumes, but your faith is especially eloquent. I'm so proud of you!

Chapter One

The sprawling old house creaked and groaned in the afternoon heat. Its cedar siding expanded with reluctant moans, while the steep, gleaming metal roof snapped impatiently beneath the relentless July sun. Such was summer in south central Oklahoma.

Having grown up here on Straight Arrow Ranch, Ann Jollett Billings found the heat of mid-July no surprise. She was used to worse, frankly, and better, having spent the past six years in Dallas, Texas, being a manager in the finest hotel that city had to offer. Despite the opulence of her usual surroundings, however, what Ann now found difficult to bear was not the utilitarian inconveniences of her childhood home but the silence.

She couldn't recall the last time that she'd had more than a few quiet hours to herself, let alone two whole days. Managing a hotel meant being on call virtually around the clock; managing a ranch, not so much, even apparently during the "busy season." At least her brother had claimed this to be the busy season before he had taken off to Tulsa with his new wife and adorable baby girl to settle personal business and put his condo on the market, leaving Ann in charge of the family ranch during his absence. She'd taken the time to fully computerize their bookkeeping, which would allow Rex to track everything online. Their sister, Meredith, a nurse, had left the afternoon after Rex, on Sunday, to take their father, Wes, to Oklahoma City for his second chemotherapy treatment. The house had been as silent as a tomb ever since.

So who was pushing a chair across the kitchen floor? That noise, Ann suddenly realized, could not be anything else.

"Oh, Lord," she prayed softly, "please don't let this be happening. Not here. Not now."

Rising from the battered old desk in her father's study, Ann crept to the door that led into the foyer and listened. The screeching stopped, but other sounds ensued. She was definitely not alone in the house. Her imagination, fueled by her years in Dallas, conjured numerous scenarios, none of them innocent. Reason told her that theft was a rare thing around the small town of

War Bonnet, Oklahoma, which lay five miles or so away. Rarer still in the outlying rural surrounds, but perhaps one of the employees of the custom cutter hired to install the new feed bins and harvest the oat and sorghum crops had assumed that, with Wes and Rex gone, the house would be empty and, therefore, easy pickings.

Well, she was no helpless female. Never had been; never would be. At five feet eight inches in height and a hundred thirty-five pounds, she had enough heft to do some damage, if necessary, though more than once she'd wished otherwise.

"All right. If this is how it has to be," she whispered, "then give me strength, give me wisdom, give me courage, and send that thief running."

Moving quietly in her expensive Gucci flats, black jeans and lace-trimmed, jade-green silk T-shirt, she eased open the door of the coat closet at the foot of the front stairs and reached inside for the baseball bat that had been stored there since her brother had left home for college twenty years earlier. She could have taken the shotgun or the rifle from the high shelf, but it had been too long since she'd used a gun. Besides, she knew how to swing a bat for maximum effect, having played four years of fast-pitch softball in high school and three in college.

Holding the bat at her side, she slunk in long, silent steps across the foyer, through the living room and dining room to the door of the kitchen, glancing out the windows as she went. She saw no new vehicles parked alongside the dusty, red-clay road that ran between the ranch house and the outbuildings that sheltered machinery, fodder and livestock, primarily the horses used to work the two-square-mile Straight Arrow Ranch. The regular hands—Woody, Cam and Duffy—lived off-site and would have simply come to the front door if they'd needed to speak to her.

She lifted the heavy wood club into position and darted through the door into the kitchen. A dog—a mottled, black-masked blue heeler with brown markings, one of the better herding dogs—wagged its tail expectantly beside a kitchen chair pushed up to the counter, atop which kneeled an impish redheaded boy with his arm buried up to the elbow in the owl-shaped cookie jar.

"Hello!" sang out the boy, his bright blue eyes hitting a chord of familiarity within her. Completely unrepentant to have been caught stealing cookies, he turned onto his bottom, pitched a cookie to his dog and crammed another into his mouth. "Mmm-mmm."

Stunned, Ann let the bat slide through her hands until she could park the butt on the floor and lean against the top. "Thank You, Lord!" she breathed. Then, in as reasonable a tone as she could muster, she demanded, "What do you think you're doing?"

He blinked at her, his freckles standing out in sharp contrast to his pale skin.

"Eatin' cookies," he answered carefully as if any dummy could see that.

His eyes were the brightest blue she'd ever seen, far brighter than her own pale, lackluster shade. He had eyes like sapphires. Hers more closely resembled the sun-bleached sky of a hot, cloudless summer noon. Suddenly she remembered where she'd seen eyes like them before, and to whom they belonged. Dean Paul Pryor. The very reason she was stuck in this dusty backcountry.

She had first met Pryor at her brother's wedding reception, when Rex had identified him as the custom cutter who would be harvesting their oat and remaining barley crops and installing the new feed storage and mixing station while Rex, his new bride, Callie, and her baby daughter were in Tulsa on a combined honeymoon and business trip. Pryor had presented himself again that morning when he'd reported for work.

Dean Paul Pryor was everything Ann disliked in a man: tall, gorgeous, confident, masculine. She suspected he stood taller than her brother, who was at least six foot two. Dean might even be as tall as her dad, at six foot four. Solidly built, he outweighed her by at least fifty pounds. Add the short, thick, wheat-blond hair, gem-like blue eyes and the square-jawed perfection of his face, and he had everything he needed to make most women melt at his feet. But not her.

He'd mentioned that morning that he had his son with him. She hadn't expected the boy to be so young, however. This child couldn't be older than six or seven.

"Where is your father?" she asked icily, taking a choke hold on the bat again.

"Workin'," came the laconic answer.

Obviously the father, as well as the son, needed to be taught some manners. Well, this wouldn't be the first spoiled brat who she'd had to deal with or the first lazy, uninvolved parent she'd had to set straight. *This* was why she didn't have children, why she never intended to have children. One of the reasons.

"Come."

Shrugging, the shameless imp helped himself to several more cookies. What he couldn't stuff into his mouth, he crammed into the pockets of his baggy jeans before hopping down onto the chair and then the floor. As she had no intention of eating the cookies or anything he'd touched, she allowed it. He began to push the chair back toward the table, its feet screeching across the wood planks.

"Leave it!" Ann ordered, her eyes crossing at the high-pitched noise.

The dog barked sharply as if in agreement, and the boy again shrugged. Ann again pointed to the door, and he happily set off, the dog falling in at his side.

"Mmm, Mizz Callie mawkz ze bezz cookeez," he said around the mass in his mouth as Ann escorted him through the house.

"Didn't anyone ever tell you not to talk with your mouth full?" she scolded, stopping to put the bat back in the closet.

Nodding, he looked up at her with those big blue eyes, gulped and said, "You sure are pretty. And you got red hair like me." He grinned suddenly, displaying an empty space in the front of his mouth where a tooth should be. "Come and meet my dad, why doncha?" With that, he turned, opened the front door and ran outside, the dog scampering after him.

Her mouth agape, Ann snatched a faded ball cap from its wall peg, a shield against the relentless summer sun and the possibility of freckles, crammed it onto her head and went after the miniature thief.

From the corner of his eye, Dean Paul Pryor caught sight of his son in the field just south of the big red barn. As previously instructed,

Donovan stopped at a safe distance to watch as Dean used the small, rented crane to drag a cone-shaped steel bin on stilts from a flatbed trailer and carefully, painstakingly stand it upright. Dean let out a sigh of relief as four workers in white hard hats guided the stilt legs of the bin to the concrete base. Donovan, meanwhile, munched his cookies and watched, rapt, as the workers settled the five-ton bin, one of several, and began bolting it down.

Smiling, Dean shook his head. He should've known that nothing, not even chocolate chip cookies, could keep the boy away from the construction zone. What red-blooded boy could resist the lure of heavy machinery and risky maneuvers? At least Donovan had sense enough to keep his distance.

Just then one of the workers dropped a fist-size nut meant for an enormous bolt. The nut bumped across the uneven ground.

The boy darted forward, yelling, "I'll get it!"

Dean's heart leaped into his throat. Abruptly letting out the clutch, he killed the engine on the old crane and bailed out of the cab, waving his arms and shouting over the sound of screeching metal as the full weight of the bin suddenly came to rest.

"Donovan! No! Get back! Get back!"

The boy froze in his tracks then began creeping backward. The worker who had dropped the nut quickly retrieved it and began threading it onto the bolt sticking up from the concrete base. Pocketing his mirrored sunglasses, Pryor strode toward the boy. To Dean's surprise, Ann Jollett Billings got to Donovan before he did, pulling the boy backward several steps. Dean temporarily ignored her.

"Son, I meant it when I told you that you couldn't help with the feed bins," he said firmly. "It's too dangerous. That's why I sent you to the house."

"You *sent* him to the house?" Ann demanded.

Dean swept off his hard hat. He never could ignore her for long, and as always she was a sight for sore eyes, especially with that familiar old baseball cap on her head.

"Hello, Jolly," he said around a grin.

She gasped. "Jolly!"

The nickname, a reference to her middle name, Jollett, had once been used by those closest to her, but Dean had momentarily forgotten that particular circle had never included *him*. The look she gave him said so in no uncertain terms, the message coming across loud and clear. He sucked in a quiet breath.

"You really don't remember me at all, do you?" he asked on a wry chuckle, scratching his nose to hide a hurt that he had no real right to feel.

She tossed her long, wavy hair off her shoulder with a flick of her hand. "Should I?"

"We went to school together."

"We did not."

"Oh, we did," Dean insisted lightly. "I was ball boy for the softball team all four years you played."

Ann stiffened. "That was you?" Obviously she didn't like being reminded of those she had once considered beneath her. "Ah. Well, you're younger than me, then."

"Not that much younger. Three years."

"A lifetime in high school," Ann retorted dismissively.

"High school," Dean said drily, "doesn't last forever. Three years makes a difference at thirteen and sixteen. Not so much at twenty-five and twenty-eight."

She lifted her pert little nose. "Matter of opinion."

Stung, as he had so often been in the past by her, he switched his attention to the boy. "Get your cookies?"

"You sent him to the house to steal cookies?" Ann yelped.

"How is it stealing," Dean asked, frowning as he plunked his hard hat onto his head again and pulled his son to stand against his legs, "when Callie left the cookies for him and told us where to find them?"

He saw the shock of that roll over her, deflating her anger, but then she lifted that stubborn chin again.

"He should at least knock."

Dean looked down at the boy. "Donovan, did you knock?"

"Yessir."

"I was sitting at the desk in the study, right next to the front door," Ann argued.

"I sent him to the *back* door," Dean Paul pointed out, "because his shoes were dusty." He looked down at Donovan again. "What did Miss Callie say you were to do if no one answered?"

"Go in and he'p myself."

Dean looked to Ann, who colored brightly even as she sniffed, "Well, no one told me."

He lifted his eyebrows to tell her that wasn't his problem. Then he looked down at his son and said, "Why don't you and Digger go explore the corrals while I take care of the big feed bin." He speared Ann with a direct, challenging look then. "If that's all right with you."

"Yes, of course," she muttered.

"Just don't go into the stables," Dean warned his son.

"Mr. Wes said it was okay."

"Yes, he did, but you're not to go in there alone. I'll take you inside to look at the horses later. Understood?"

"Yessir." The boy reached into his pocket and produced a cookie for his father. Despite the boy's grimy hands and the melting chocolate, Dean took it and bit off a huge chunk.

"Yum."

"Don't tell Grandma," Donovan said in a husky whisper, "but Mizz Callie makes the best cookies."

Dean held a finger to his lips, but the boy was already running toward the big red barn and the maze of corrals beyond it. Smiling, Dean polished off the remainder of the cookie in a single large bite.

"He may be right," Dean mused after swallowing. "All I know is that they're really good. Don't you agree?"

Ann jerked slightly. Then she nodded, shook her head, nodded again. "I'm sure they are."

He swept his gaze over her. "You haven't even tried them."

Was she that vain now, this polished, sophisticated version of the fun, competitive girl he used to know—and admire? Did that svelte figure and the fit of those pricey clothes matter more to her now than a little sugar, a moment's enjoyment? Oddly, it hurt him to think it, but it was none of his business. Nothing about her had ever been any of his business, much as he might have wished it otherwise.

"He's awfully young to be out here with you, isn't he?" she asked pointedly.

"Donovan's been coming into the field with me since he was toilet trained," Dean informed her. "I figure he's safer with me than anywhere else. I always know where he is and what he's doing. Besides, I want him with me. The day's fast coming when he can't be."

"I see. Well, it's your business."

"It is that."

"And I don't care for sweets," Ann called defensively as he turned away and began to trudge toward the newly installed feed bin, plucking his sunglasses from his shirt pocket.

"It shows," he drawled, and not just in her trim figure. Her attitude could use some sweetening, in his opinion, but he couldn't fault her shape.

Telling himself to put her out of mind as he had so often done before, he strode to the feed bin, climbed the attached metal ladder and began releasing the chains with which he had hoisted the heavy, white-painted steel bin into place. Tomorrow he would begin harvesting the oats that would be stored in this particular bin.

The second bin—this one painted green—was even larger and would contain the sorghum crop. This, too, Dean would harvest, but only after the oats were in, as much more heat would strip the oats of their protein content. After that, a blending plant would be built.

Rex and Wes Billings had decided to take the ranch onto an organic pathway. Wes had started the process months ago when he'd allowed Dean to plant and oversee the two forage crops without any pesticides. To Dean's surprise, Rex had even given up his law practice in Tulsa to permanently move home to the Straight Arrow Ranch and oversee the transition, while his dad received treatment for his cancer. Wes imagined that Rex's wife, Callie, had something to do with that decision.

If Rex was happy living on the Straight Arrow and practicing law in War Bonnet, the tiny Oklahoma town where he, Ann and their younger sister, Meredith, had all gone to school, then Dean wished him well, but he couldn't imagine that Ann would follow suit. She had long ago let her disdain be known for this community and everyone in it, himself included, not that she'd ever seemed to know he was alive until now.

So why, Dean wondered, did he feel particularly slighted? Why had Ann Billings always had the power to wound him?

* * *

Ann marched across the pasture to the road. Red-orange dust settled on the toes of her buttery, pale leather flats as she crossed the hard-packed dirt road that ran between the big sagging red barn and the house. She told herself that Dean Pryor's disdain meant nothing to her. Why should it? He was just another local yokel. She'd barely noticed him in high school—and yet now that she thought about it, he'd always been there on the periphery during what she thought of as her jock phase.

Memories of that time in her life made Ann mentally cringe. She hadn't stopped to think back then that being able to compete with her brother, out-swinging half the guys on the baseball team and generally acting like a tomboyish hoyden would mark her as less than feminine. Her middle name, which she shared with her mother and grandmother, had been a source of pride for her, even when the coach who'd given her extra batting practice with the boys' baseball team had shortened Jollett to "Jolly" and the nickname had stuck. It hadn't occurred to her that being seen as "one of the guys" would literally mean being seen as one of the guys. Even now, though, all these years later, she couldn't seem to outlive either the nickname or the impression.

Around War Bonnet and the Straight Arrow, she was Jolly Billings, the mannish, unfeminine daughter of Wes Billings, and nothing she could do would change that. No matter that she rose every morning at daylight and ran for miles to keep her figure. Never mind that she spent hours every day on her makeup and hair or wore the finest Manolo Blahnik shoes and Escada suits, not that the clodhoppers around here even knew the difference.

No, she didn't belong here, could never again belong here. Suddenly she longed for the anonymous, frenetic energy of Dallas and the quiet, reserved presence of her fiancé, Jordan Teel. At 41, Jordan was thirteen years her senior, but then Ann had always been mature for her age. That, she told herself, was why she had forgotten Dean Pryor, the younger batboy for the softball team.

She heard the phone ringing before she got back to the house and hurried inside to find her brother calling. Pushing aside thoughts of Dean Pryor, she took notes as Rex advised her of the contractors who would soon be journeying from Ardmore and Duncan to bid on building a garage behind the house and remodeling the master bedroom for him and Callie. Ann promised to take the bids, scan them and email them to him.

As they talked, she heard Donovan's high-pitched voice outside, speaking to his dog, Digger. Before long, Ann mused, her little niece, Bodie Jane, would be running around the place much like Donovan did now. That was what she and Rex had done. They'd run wild, practically living on horseback and knocking out every step their dad had taken around the place until school had intruded.

Being the youngest, Meredith had spent more time with their mom, Gloria, but Ann had desperately wanted to do everything that Rex and Wes had done. That, no doubt, had been her downfall.

Unbidden, other words ran through Ann's mind.

You sure are pretty. And you got red hair like me.

At least Donovan thought she was pretty, and it seemed to matter that she had red hair like him.

Not that she cared one way or another what the Pryors thought.

She yanked off the ball cap and touched a hand to her long, stiffly waving locks, wondering when its shade had ever before been a plus for her. She wished Callie had told her that she'd given the kid free run of the house before she'd taken off to Tulsa with Rex and Bodie. Maybe then she wouldn't have come off so…tough.

Maybe she'd have had a chance to appear soft and womanly.

On the other hand, Dean Pryor had known her a lot longer than she'd realized. She'd probably never be able to overcome the image of her hard-slugging, hard-driving, super-competitive past with him.

Not that it mattered. Actually, it didn't matter one whit what he or anyone else around War Bonnet thought of her.

Jolly.

She shook her head. It had been a long time since anyone had called her that.

Not long enough.

Chapter Two

"Watch it, Dean!"

"Sorry."

So much for *not* thinking of Ann Billings. Dean Paul pulled his attention back to the job at hand, getting the lift chains on the feed bin released without braining any of his help or injuring himself. A man could easily lose a finger if he didn't focus. Besides, what did it matter? He'd never been anything but an underclassman to her, and he was still obviously underclass in her estimation.

He could live with her low opinion of him, but it burned him up that she'd thought his son had been stealing cookies. Dean had learned to swallow his anger and focus on his joy a long time ago. Nevertheless, he couldn't help wanting to give her a piece of his mind where his boy was concerned. He listened as he worked and caught the sound of his son talking to his dog in the distance. The exact words escaped him, but the tone of Donovan's voice assured Dean that all was well. His five-year-old son, born Christmas Day, was the gift of a lifetime, in Dean's opinion.

Smiling, he released the last heavy link and let the chain fall, calling, "Heads up!" He tossed the heavy, locking S hook to the ground and descended the ladder.

When Rex had told him that Ann would be here to oversee and help with the build-out and harvest, Dean had felt a secret thrill of anticipation, but apparently nothing had changed in the last decade. She still obviously thought she was too good for the likes of him. And maybe she was. God knew that he'd made more than his fair share of mistakes in this life already.

Being a father to his son was not one of them, however. Being Donovan's dad had shown Dean that he could do anything that he had to do. It had also given him more joy than he had known the world could contain. That was all he needed, more than he'd ever expected, enough to keep him thanking God every day.

No matter how hard things got, Dean would thank God for Donovan Jessup Pryor. Those sparkling blue eyes and that happy smile gave Dean's life purpose. That little red head warmed

Dean's heart as nothing else could. He just wished he had better answers for the inevitable questions that Donovan had begun to ask.

How come I don't have a mom?

Why don't she want us?

Dean had asked those same questions his whole life and still had no satisfactory answers for them. Grandmothers and aunts were wonderful, but they weren't mothers. At least Donovan had a father who loved and wanted him. At least he'd been able to give his son that much.

It was more than Dean had had.

Hopefully it would be enough, for Dean didn't see himself marrying anytime soon. He could barely afford to feed himself and Donovan, let alone a wife and any other children. In a perfect world, he'd like a half dozen more kids.

But Dean Paul Pryor's world had never approached anything near perfect. The closest he'd ever come was the day a nurse had placed a tiny, redheaded bundle in his arms and exclaimed, "Merry Christmas!"

He had wept for joy that day, and the memory still made him smile.

What was another snub, even one from Ann Jollett Billings, in the light of that?

He shook his head and got back to work. The men helped Dean chain up the first of ten-ton storage bins and connect it to the crane. Then

Dean climbed into the cab of the crane and started the engine. Donovan and Digger showed up again, the boy's curiosity alive on his freckled face. He grinned and waved, showing the empty space where he'd knocked out his baby tooth jumping from the tire swing in their front yard. Dean sighed, torn between satisfying that little boy's love of all things mechanical and keeping his kid at a safe distance.

His first instinct was always to keep Donovan as close as possible, and soon that would no longer be close enough. Donovan would start kindergarten in a month, and their days of constant companionship would come to an end. Sighing, Dean killed the engine on the old crane once again and climbed down out of the cab. He walked to his pickup truck and extracted a hard hat and a 40-pound sandbag then waved to the ever-hopeful boy.

Donovan darted across the field, stumbling slightly on the uneven ground, the cuffs of his oversize jeans dragging in the dirt. He'd torn the pocket on his striped polo shirt. Grandma would have to mend it before putting it into the wash. His socks would never be white again but a pale, muddy, pinkish orange. He needed boots for playing out here in these red dirt fields, but he grew so fast that Dean dared not spend the money for them. The dog loped along behind him, its pink tongue lolling from its mouth.

Dean patted the side of the truck bed, commanding, "Digger, up!" Obediently, the dog launched himself into the bed of the truck. "Stay."

Panting, the heeler hung its front paws over the side of the truck, watching as Dean adjusted the liner of the hard hat and plunked it onto Donovan's head.

"I could use a little help with these big bins."

Donovan's smile could not have grown wider. "Yessir."

Dean lifted the sandbag onto his shoulder and walked with his son to the crane. Reaching inside, Dean pushed down the jump seat in the rear corner of the cab. Then he tossed the sandbag into the opposite corner before lifting Donovan onto the jump seat and belting him down.

"Sit on your hands," he instructed, "and keep your feet still."

Donovan tucked his hands under his thighs and crossed his ankles. Nodding approval, Dean climbed up into the operator's seat again.

"Keep still now," he cautioned again as he started the engine once more.

So far as he could tell, the boy didn't move a muscle as Dean guided the crane to lift the feed bin from the tractor trailer, swing it across the open ground, position it and carefully lower it, guided by the hands of his temporary crew, into place. Thankfully the job took only one try. When the chains at last went slack, Donovan hooted with glee. Dean glanced over his shoulder, smiling.

A wide smile split his son's freckled face, but he sat still as a statue. Dean's heart swelled with pride, both because the boy was truly well behaved and because he had derived such pleasure from watching the process. Dean killed the engine and swiveled the seat to pat the boy's knee. "Good job."

"That was so cool!" Donovan swung his arm, demonstrating how the steel bin had swung through the air, complete with sound effects.

Chuckling, Dean slid down to the ground. "Stay put. We've got two more to do."

After all three bins were in place and secured, Dean released his son's belt and lifted him down from the crane cab.

"You're the best oparader!" Donovan declared.

"I'm an adequate crane operator," Dean said. "Couldn't have done it without you." He leaned inside to grab the sandbag with which he'd balanced his son's weight, hefting the bag onto his shoulder once more.

Still wearing his hard hat, Donovan proudly walked back to the pickup truck with his father. "I helped, Digger," Donovan told his dog.

Caramel-brown ears flicking against his mottled dark gray head, the animal waited for a discernible command. Dean dumped the sandbag into the bed of the truck and ruffled the dog's fur before snapping his fingers next to his thigh to let the dog know he could hop down. The dog vaulted lightly to the ground.

"Why don't you guys go play in the shade while I load the crane onto the trailer?" Dean said, pointing to the trees in front of the house across the road.

"Can't I help?" Donovan whined.

"Not this time," Dean told him, taking the boy's hard hat. "I think I remember a swing on the porch. I'm sure it's okay if you and Digger want to swing for a bit. Then, after I talk to Miss Ann, we'll go look at the horses."

Donovan dug the toe of his shoe into the dirt. "O-kay."

"Sure is hot out here," Dean said, lifting off his own hat to mop his brow with the red cloth plucked from his hip pocket. "You need to be in the shade. Maybe we can stop for a snow cone on the way home."

Donovan's eyes lit up. He loved the sweet, icy treats, especially the coconut-flavored ones that turned his mouth blue.

"Yay! Come on, Digger." They ran across the dusty road and into the trees.

Dean sighed. Cookies and snow cones. They'd be dealing with a sugar high this evening for sure. Well, five-year-old boys hardly ever stopped moving. He'd burn it off before bedtime. Besides, Donovan was a good eater. The only vegetables he wouldn't touch were Brussels sprouts and cooked greens. Big for his age, he was pretty much a bottomless pit already.

Dean shuddered to think what it was going to take to feed his son at fifteen. He worried that they might have to move away from War Bonnet for him to make a decent living, but most of his work came during harvest time, and even with Oklahoma's elongated season, he hadn't yet been able to make those earnings comfortably stretch through the whole year.

Putting aside those thoughts, he went back to work, thankful that Rex Billings had tapped him for this extra job. Soon he had the rented crane loaded. While the crew chained it down so that it was ready for pick-up, he traded his hard hat for the clean, pale straw cowboy hat that his grandma had bought him for his birthday just two weeks earlier. Then he walked to the house, weary to the bone, to get payment from Ann. After showing Donovan the horses, he'd drive straight to the bank with her check, deposit it and pay his help.

When he stepped onto the porch, he found

Donovan and Digger on the cushioned swing, Donovan singing softly as he pushed them both. The boy started to get up, but Dean waved him back as he stepped up to the door.

"I'll only be a few minutes. You stay right there."

"Okay, Dad."

Dean opened the screen door and rapped his knuckles against the heavily carved inner door. After only moments Ann stood frowning up at him. He didn't know what she had to be unhappy about or why she seemed intent on taking it out on him. Her grumpiness did not, unfortunately, detract from her looks.

She had an unusual face, a longish rectangle with a squarish jaw and chin, prominent cheekbones and a high forehead. It was the sort of face that could have been outfitted with features from either gender, but hers were unmistakably feminine, from her perfect lips to her dainty, straight nose and the gentle curves of her slender brows over her big, exotic eyes. Those eyes were like orbs plucked from a clear blue sky, ringed in storm gray around shiny black pupils. They suited her as nothing else could have. He'd always thought her one of the most beautiful girls, even when she'd had freckles splattered across her nose and cheeks. He kind of missed those freckles.

Aware that he was staring, he cleared his throat. "All done for now."

She inclined her head, her red hair sliding across her face. Of a more muted shade than Donovan's, more golden, less orange, it glistened like copper pennies. Dean frowned. Hadn't her hair been brighter at one time? He fought the insane urge to rub locks of it between his fingers to see if the color rubbed off and exposed the brighter hue he seemed to recall.

Turning, she led the way into the study where he had conducted his business with her father and brother. Dean lifted off his hat, stepped inside, pushed the door closed behind him and followed. Leaning over the desk, she signed a check, tore it from a large, hard-backed checkbook and handed it over.

"I really didn't know about the cookies," she said defensively. "Callie didn't tell me."

He glanced at the check, folded it and stashed it in his shirt pocket. "I suppose she had a lot on her mind, what with the wedding and all."

The young widowed mother had come to keep house for the Billings men and help take care of Wes, who was fighting cancer. It had quickly become obvious to everyone who saw them together that she and Ann's brother, Rex, were made for each other. They had married within weeks.

Ann dropped down into the chair behind the desk, muttering, "I suppose. I don't really see what the rush was, though."

Surprised, Dean lifted his brows at that. "Don't you?"

"No," she stated flatly, laying both of her hands on the desk blotter. "I don't."

He saw the big diamond on her left hand then, and understanding dawned. Along with unwelcome disappointment. "Ah. And how long have you been engaged?"

"Not long," she said, smiling and leaning back in the desk chair, "but I don't intend to rush things. A proper wedding takes time to plan."

His throat burned with a sudden welling of acid. "Does it? I thought Rex and Callie's wedding was everything *proper*."

"You know what I mean."

"No. Sorry, I don't."

Ann rolled her pale eyes. "Well, for starters, I won't be getting married *here*."

He nodded, an ugly bitterness surging inside him. "Got it. War Bonnet's not good enough for you."

Blinking, she rose to her feet. "No, that's not it at all. It's just that the majority of my friends and most of my business contacts live in Dallas now."

"Uh-huh."

She folded her arms. "What's that supposed to mean?"

"Nothing. Just…" He really needed to shut his mouth and get out of there. Instead, he said, "You haven't changed much, have you? Except you're coloring your hair now." He knew it suddenly, and she confirmed it by lifting a hand to her hair, something like guilt flashing across her face.

"What do you mean, I haven't changed? I've changed a lot."

"No, you haven't," he said, knowing he was being rude but unable to help himself for some reason. "You're still a snob."

She jerked as if he'd hit her. "I am *not* a snob."

"Really? Couldn't prove it by me." He might as well still be the ball boy to her athletic highness.

"What do *you* have to do with it?" she demanded.

"Not a thing," he told her, thumping his hat onto his head and turning away.

"And what's wrong with my hair?" she demanded.

He looked back at her. "I like the real you better, that's all."

"You don't know the real me," she snapped.

He let his gaze sweep over her, liking what he

saw, missing what he didn't see, wishing otherwise on both counts.

"Don't I?" he asked. "You still look and act like the queen of War Bonnet High to me."

With that, he finally got out of there, calling himself ten kinds of fool. The queen, after all, couldn't be expected to do more than barely acknowledge her servants.

Calling herself the very worst kind of fool, Ann guided her father's pickup truck off the dusty road and over the rough cattle guard between the pipes supporting the fencing. She didn't know why she'd come. Rex had told her simply to make sure that Dean could get his equipment in and out of the field without problem. As the weather had remained hot and dry, Dean could have had no issues whatsoever, so she really had no reason to trek out here and inspect the job site. His rudeness the day before should have been reason enough to forgo this particular chore, and yet she'd found herself dressing with ridiculous detail for an encounter she had no desire to make. Why should she care what he thought of her, after all? Yet, here she was in all her feminine glory, including denim leggings, a matching tank top and a formfitting, crocheted cardigan that perfectly matched her white high-heeled sandals.

Dean had obviously taken down a section of the barbed wire in order to get his combine into the field. He was even now using a come-along to draw the post back into position, the wires still attached, so he could temporarily restore the fence. Ann beeped the truck's horn to stop him then killed the engine and got out.

Watching her pick her way across the ground on her high heels, he let the wire stretcher drop, stripped off his leather gloves and took off his sunglasses, dropping them into his shirt pocket. The hard hat had been replaced by a faded red baseball cap, which he tugged lower over his eyes. Dirt gritted between her toes as she made her way toward him, but she refused to show any discomfort. At least the early-morning temperature wouldn't melt her carefully applied makeup or frizz her hair, which she'd painstakingly set on heated curlers after her shower and predawn run. Resisting the urge to tug on the hem of her tank top, she plastered on a smile and tucked her muted red hair behind one ear so he could see the dainty pearl earrings she was wearing.

"I meant to tell you yesterday," she announced. "Rex had the hands move all the cattle to the east range, so you don't have to worry about replacing the fence until you're done here."

He glanced around, his gaze landing on her feet. "Okay. Good to know. Thanks."

She heard barking a second before Digger shot out of the thigh-high golden oats, a yellow bandanna clenched in his doggy teeth. Giggling wildly, Donovan careened behind him. The dog skidded to a halt, facing Donovan, who snatched at the bandanna. Turning, the dog took off again, making straight for Ann and Dean. Before either could react, the animal bolted between them and came to a taunting halt just beyond. Shrieking with laughter, Donovan gave chase. Right across Ann's toes.

"Ow!" Yelping in pain, she reeled backward.

Dean lurched forward, grabbing her by the arms and pulling her into his embrace even as he scolded the boy. "Donovan Jessup! Watch what you're doing."

The child immediately sobered, turning to face the adults. "I'm sorry."

Ann staggered against Dean, her elbow digging into his side, his very solid side. His large, heavy hands cupped her other elbow and clamped her waist, steadying her. Those were the hands of a real man, strong, capable, sure. She felt dainty, safe and cherished in that moment.

"You okay?"

Aware that her heartbeat raced, she ignored her throbbing toes to smile and nod. "Yes. Thank you."

"Good," he said, dropping his arms and stepping back. "Next time you come out here, maybe you'll wear boots."

Ann gasped, her silly illusions abruptly shattered. "And maybe you'll control that wild thing you call a child," she snapped, regretting the words the moment they escaped her mouth.

Dean's expression instantly hardened. "Let me walk you to your truck," he stated firmly.

Setting her jaw, Ann intended to refuse—until she caught sight of Donovan's face. The dismay on that small, freckled face smacked her right in the chest. She bit back the caustic reply on the tip of her tongue and allowed Dean to clamp his large, hard hand around her arm just above her elbow. They moved across the ground in silence. She teetered and danced across the uneven terrain while he strode purposefully along beside her.

When they reached the truck, he opened the driver's door and all but tossed her up behind the wheel before stepping close, looking her straight in the eye and commanding flatly, "Don't ever speak that way in front of my son again."

"I won't," she capitulated softly. "I'm sorry."

Dean relaxed a bit and sucked in a calming breath. "He's five. He makes mistakes, but he's a good boy. He'd have apologized again if you'd given him a chance."

She nodded. "I was just…hurt. And I didn't realize that he's so young."

Dean shifted until he was halfway inside the cab, draping his left arm over the top of the steering wheel. "He's big for his age, I admit." He rubbed a hand over his face before asking, "Your toes okay?"

For some reason she couldn't seem to breathe as easily as she ought to, but she managed to squeak, "I think so."

"Next time," he said quietly, pointedly, "wear boots."

"Don't you like my shoes?" she asked, truly curious about that.

A crease appeared between his brows. "What's that got to do with anything?" Angling his head, he looked down at the floorboard. "Your shoes are fine. That's not the point." He looked her in the eye, adding, "If you're going to come out here, you need the proper footwear."

"Unfortunately, I only have dress shoes and running shoes."

"Well, you better go shopping, then."

"In War Bonnet?"

He chuckled. "Most of us drive to Ardmore or Duncan or even Lawton or Oklahoma City."

"That's more than an hour away!"

"I'm told that it can take more than an hour to drive across Dallas."

He had her there. "True. But I know where to shop in Dallas, and I wouldn't have to drive across town to do it."

Shrugging, he backed out of the cab and straightened. "Risk your toes, then. Just don't say I didn't warn you."

Great, she thought. So much for showing her feminine side.

She just could not win with this guy. No matter what she did, it turned out wrong. She didn't know why it mattered.

Somehow, though, it did matter. A lot.

Still, she had a job to do here, and she was all about doing the job. That, at least, she could manage. If she needed boots to do the job, she'd figure out how to get her hands on a pair of boots. Couldn't be that difficult. Right?

Chapter Three

Ann had once owned numerous pairs of boots, but she'd thrown them all away, convinced that such masculine attire should no longer be tolerated. She wondered if her sister had done the same, however. Long ago she and Meri had worn the same size shoes. In fact, they'd worn the same size everything, then Ann had experienced a sudden growth spurt during her freshman year in high school and shot up several inches. Everyone had expected Meredith to follow suit, but she never had. Still, looking in Meri's closet was worth a shot.

Though Meredith's surviving cat had traveled to Oklahoma City with Meri and their father, Ann opened the door to her sister's bedroom with some trepidation. Meredith had an apartment in the city and, while on temporary leave at the moment, worked as a nurse in the very hospital where Wes was even now receiving his che-motherapy. Generous to a fault and sweet, Meri was, nevertheless, manic about her cats, one of which had been accidentally killed on the day of Rex's wedding.

Her room showed her obsession. Every kind of cat contraption imaginable filled the space. Connecting tubes, scratching posts, toys, feeding stations and an elaborate litter pan/carrier thingy. Meri even had framed photos of her cats, including the dead one. Meredith still blamed the local veterinarian for not saving the poor thing. Ann certainly would not have done away with the cat, but one cat per house seemed quite adequate to her. Meredith claimed that Ann just didn't understand, and Ann supposed that was true. She was more of a dog person, really.

The intelligent face of Donovan Pryor's dog came to mind with its perky, twitching ears and alert black eyes. That dog certainly seemed smart and playful, a great companion for a little boy.

This space was too small for the amount of cat junk crammed into it, Ann noted. There was hardly room enough for the bed.

After searching her sister's closet, Ann found three pairs of Western boots. All proved too small, so she reluctantly accepted defeat before carefully closing the bedroom door behind her.

Her next step took her into War Bonnet, but Mrs. Burton's Soft Goods had long since closed, and the local grocery sent her to the Feed and Grain, which offered nothing more than work gloves and tool belts. She stopped at the gas station to refuel her BMW coupe for the drive out of town, and that was where she ran into the one person she had most hoped to avoid.

Jack Lyons had been a fixture at War Bonnet High for at least two decades. So far as Ann knew, he had never married. All indications were that he ate, drank and slept sports. Yet it was common knowledge that he had turned down positions with much larger school districts, and for that he was greatly revered by the local populace. Coach Lyons had spotted Ann's athleticism early on, but he hadn't offered her extra batting practice until she'd buckled down and gotten serious about improving her stats and landing a softball scholarship. The extra practice had meant working out with several of the guys on the baseball team.

Those practice sessions had involved lots of teasing and laughter, but Ann hadn't cared. Like every other kid who played for Lyons, his respect meant everything to her. She hadn't always managed to hold her own against the guys, but she'd done so often enough to be good-natured about it when she failed. This had prompted Lyons to tag her with the Jolly nickname, a play on her middle name, Jollett. Ann had done her best to live up to the label.

Under his tutelage, the softball team had won their district championship four years in a row, with Ann as the team's number-one slugger. Coach Lyons had written her glowing recommendations, and she'd managed to win a minor scholarship to Southeastern State in Durant, where she'd studied business management and marketing. For the next three years she'd driven home as often as she could, and she'd never failed to stop by the school and say hello to Coach Lyons. He'd always seemed happy to see her. Then, near the end of her junior year, she'd stopped by the field house just in time to overhear a conversation between Lyons and another teacher.

"Saw Ann Billings pull into the parking lot a minute ago." It had sounded, strangely, as if the other teacher, Caroline Carmody, was warning Coach.

He had sighed and said, "Guess that means she'll be here soon."

Ann had paused beside his office door to listen, puzzled.

"What's the deal with her?" Caroline had asked. "She's been out of school for years. Why is she still coming around?"

"The awkward ones are like that sometimes," the coach had opined.

"You think she's awkward?" Caroline had asked.

Jack Lyons had snorted. "She's taller than half the male population. She could outhit most of the teenage boys I've worked with, and if you cut off her hair, I'm not sure you could tell the difference."

Horrified, Ann had slapped a hand over her own mouth to keep from crying out in pain.

"It's true she's not the most feminine girl I've ever known," Caroline had said with a chortle. "If she comes back to War Bonnet after college, she'll probably wind up an old maid out on that ranch with her mom and dad."

Lyons said something else, but Ann hadn't stayed around to listen. She'd run as quickly and quietly from the field house as possible.

Some serious thinking had followed, and her conclusions had been painful.

Her parents had not encouraged her to date during high school, and the pickings around War Bonnet had seemed slim at best, especially once she'd started outdoing many of the guys at sports. For most of her college career, she'd focused on academics, sports and working enough to help her parents afford tuition and expenses. Her disinterest in partying had ruled out a great many prospective dating partners, but she hadn't worried about it. Now, suddenly, she wondered if something might be fundamentally wrong with her, if she was seriously lacking in the feminine qualities necessary to attract male interest.

Horrified by the future painted for her by Coach Lyons and the teacher, Caroline Carmody, she had taken steps to ensure that she would never be War Bonnet's pathetic spinster. Telling her family that she wanted to focus on hotel management, she had transferred to the University of North Texas for her senior year. The move had required her to give up her scholarship, take several extra classes and delay graduation until the age of twenty-two, but she'd made up for all that with hard work and early success in her field.

She'd told only one other soul about the fears she'd nursed for so long.

Her fiancé Jordan's only response at the time had been to say that War Bonnet's loss was Luxury HotelInc's gain. Later, when he'd proposed, Jordan had reminded her that no one in War Bonnet could possibly value her as much as he and LHI did.

Ann had successfully avoided conversation with Jack Lyons until that very morning at the gas station. Jack climbed up out of his vintage Mustang and reached for the gas nozzle. He'd put on a bit of weight, but he still looked almost exactly like he had the day he'd impacted her life. His gaze slid over Ann on the opposite side of the pump with a friendly, disinterested nod then came back for a second look.

"Jolly!" he exclaimed, making Ann cringe.

"Coach," she returned quietly, willing the slow old pump to fill the coupe tank faster.

Lyons walked around the pump to take a long look at the coupe.

"Very nice. Series 4?"

She nodded.

"I always knew you'd make good," he said, smiling. "You still in Dallas?"

"Yes. I manage a hotel there."

His gaze raked over the car again. "Big, fancy hotel, I imagine."

"You could say that. I, uh, I understand you're head coach now."

"Athletic director," he corrected proudly.

She put on a smile. "Ah. Congratulations."

"Thanks. How's your dad? Heard he's been ill."

She nodded. "Undergoing chemotherapy."

"Oh, I'm sorry to hear it."

"I'll tell him you asked about him."

Lifting her arms, she swept her hair back with both hands, trying not to fidget beneath his stare.

"Is that an engagement ring I see, or have you

taken to wearing a house on your finger?" he quipped.

Feeling rather smug about it, Ann straightened the cushion-cut diamond. "I am engaged, as a matter of fact."

"Congratulations. Dallas boy?"

"Not a boy," Ann said pointedly, "and not from Dallas, at least not originally. He's actually from New Hampshire, though he's moved around a lot. Right now he's filling in for me while I'm here helping out."

"So you're coworkers, then."

"Not exactly. He used to be my boss. Now he's upper management in another area of the company."

"So when you're married you'll be living where?"

"I'm not exactly sure," she admitted. "Jordan is working that out with the company now."

"Won't be in War Bonnet, though, will it?"

"No. It won't be in War Bonnet."

Jack nodded. "Well, don't be a stranger."

The fuel pump clicked off. Ann turned away with a sense of satisfaction mingled with relief, saying, "I'll try not to. I really need to get going now."

He pushed away from the truck. "Important doings, huh?"

"Boot shopping."

"Ah. Where you headed?"

"Duncan, I suppose." Ann replaced the cap on the neck of the gas tank.

"Try the Western wear store on 81," he advised.

"Okay."

"Good seeing you," he said, wandering back toward his vehicle.

Smiling, Ann climbed into the car, started up the engine and drove away, thinking how odd it was that the man who had so impacted her life would never know how he had changed things for her. Had she not overheard that conversation that day, she might well have finished school, come back to War Bonnet and…what? She'd had some vague notion of taking over the ranch at some point, but other than that…

For some reason, Dean Pryor's face sprang up before her mind's eye, so real in that instant that she gasped.

Heart pounding, she shook her head. Dean Paul Pryor was nothing to her. He could never be anything to her. Why, he didn't even compare to Jordan.

She told herself that was because Jordan existed on an entirely different plane than the men in War Bonnet. He was suave, polished, always expertly groomed. She'd never seen him in anything other than a classically tailored suit. Jordan's idea of casual wear was a suit without a tie, but even then he tended to favor silk T-shirts in place of his usual handmade dress shirts. She wondered if he even owned a pair of jeans. He must. They'd been friends for years, and she'd seen photos of him swimming and skiing. Surely he didn't wade up out of the ocean or come down off the slopes only to relax in a nice three-piece, Italian wool suit. It was just that most of their interactions had taken place in more formal surroundings.

Truthfully, Ann didn't have much of a life outside the hotel. Being on call twenty-four hours a day, seven days a week put a damper on a girl's social life. That was why she and Jordan had become friends in the first place; she just didn't have a lot of other options.

When Jordan had returned to Dallas to temporarily take over for her during her leave of absence so she could help her father through this health challenge, Jordan had immediately confessed that he'd formed feelings for her when he'd been her boss that had gone beyond friendship. He'd declared that he meant to sweep her off her feet, and then he'd done just that. In the three weeks they'd had to bring him up to speed on the current operations of the hotel before she'd left for Oklahoma, they'd become engaged.

Strangely, however, Jordan, Dallas and the

hotel no longer seemed quite real. Instead, Dean Pryor, War Bonnet and the Straight Arrow were her current reality. Surely it was natural, then, to compare Jordan to Dean.

And yet, she could not bring herself to do it. She simply refused to compare her fiancé to Dean Pryor in any way. She didn't even want to know why.

"Yep, those are boots, all right," Dean pronounced, staring down at Ann's feet on Friday morning. He was very glad that he'd kept his sunglasses on after she'd driven up and gotten out of the truck, for he feared that she'd have read in his eyes exactly what he thought of those pink-and-pearl-white, pointed-toe monstrosities.

Apparently he didn't cover his opinion up well enough, because she brought her hands to her shapely hips and demanded, "What's wrong with them?"

"Nothing!" he exclaimed, shaking his head. "They'll protect your toes out here just fine."

She frowned at the rounded toes of his scuffed, brown leather boots then tilted her head, obviously comparing her own footwear with his. Her boots were designed for riding, with toes so sharp that they almost curled upward at the tips. She had clearly chosen them based on color and style rather than function, but he wouldn't embarrass her by saying so. Unfortunately, Cam wasn't that circumspect.

One of the longtime hands at Straight Arrow Ranch, Cam had evidently known Ann from childhood. How else could he have gotten away with calling her pet names?

"You always did like fancy duds, Freckles," Cam declared, strolling up to the harvester where Dean and Ann stood talking. "Oo-ee! You bought them boots right outta the window of the Western wear store up there in Duncan, didn't you? Why, them things been there nigh on thirty years, I reckon." He grinned at Dean, shaking his head. "Just goes to show that something'll come back in style if you wait long enough, don't it?"

Dean kept his jaw clamped and rubbed his nose, while Ann turned red. She lifted her chin and seemed about to turn on her heel when Donovan ran up behind her. He just naturally threw his arms around her thighs and hugged her, startling a high, shocked yip out of her. To Donovan, anyone he saw more than twice was a close, personal friend.

"Hello!" he sang, swinging around her body as if she were a maypole, a long-legged maypole wearing hideous boots.

She recovered quickly, smiled and smoothed a hand across Donovan's back. "Hello. Where's your dog?"

For an answer, Donovan put his head back and yelled, "Digger!" The dog bolted from somewhere to the boy's side. "Here he is."

"That's one fine dog," Cam declared enviously. "Show her what he can do."

Thinking that it might take her mind off the boots and Donovan's unorthodox greeting, Dean complied. He put Digger through a series of tricks then nodded to Donovan.

"Ready?" Donovan fell to his knees. "Digger, protect!" Dean commanded.

Instantly the dog knocked the boy to the ground and stood over him with all four legs, growling, teeth bared, while Donovan lay still beneath the animal.

"Digger, safe!" Dean said.

The dog moved to sit beside the boy, its tongue lolling happily from its mouth. Donovan hugged and petted the dog, crooning softly to it.

"That's amazing," Ann said.

"Wish I had me a dog like that," Cam said, not for the first time. "You ought to think about training dogs for a living, Dean."

Dean chuckled. "Not much call for that around here, I imagine."

"I'm not so sure about that," Ann said. "Lots of local farmers and ranchers use herding dogs. They might be interested in the kind of protective training Digger has."

Dean shrugged. "You can't train just the dog. You have to train the owner, too."

Donovan got up, and Dean went to dust him off, but Ann reached him before Dean did.

"How does your mama manage your laundry?" she asked, ruffling his hair.

"Don't got a mama," Donovan announced baldly. "Grandma does my laundry."

"And a chore it is, too," Dean said quickly, whacking dirt from Donovan's bottom. "Run and get the water jug now. We've got work to do."

Donovan nodded, but he stood looking up at Ann for a second longer. "I like your boots," he said before taking off with Digger on his heels.

"Thank you," she called after him, turning a wry smile on Dean. He had to clear his throat and swallow to keep from laughing as he turned toward the cab of the harvester.

Cam said, "That reminds me. I need to check the water in the east range." He ambled off toward the four-wheeler that Rex had recently purchased.

Dean traded his cowboy hat for the ball cap then turned toward the combine. To his surprise, he felt Ann's hand on his shoulder. He turned his head to find her biting her lip.

"Um, obviously I could use some…guidance."

Guidance. Somehow he thought this could be

a momentous admission for Ann Jollett Billings. Letting go of the rails, he turned to face her.

"About?"

She looked down at her toes then up at him. "I've been away from the ranch for a long time. Obviously I don't have a clue about what boots to buy."

The grin he'd been trying to hold back since she'd first climbed out of her dad's old truck broke free at last. "They sure saw you coming, didn't they?"

She smacked him in the shoulder, which made him laugh. Then she laughed, too.

"They were in the window. I thought they were the latest style. I didn't even look at anything else."

"I hope they were cheap, at least."

"I don't know." She told him what she'd paid, and he nodded.

"Cheap enough." He considered a moment and made a decision. "I've got to take Donovan shopping for school supplies tomorrow. If you want to come along, we'll see about getting you into a proper pair of boots."

"Oh, I don't want to intrude."

"Donovan would love it if you came," Dean pointed out, "especially as Digger will have to stay home." He shook his head. "The truth is, I'm not sure how he's going to manage school without Digger. Donovan was eighteen months old when we got that dog. I'm having to find ways to wean them apart."

"I see. Well, if you're sure."

"I'll work till noon," he told her. "Then we'd planned to grab lunch in town and go shopping after that. Sound okay to you?"

To his surprise, she nodded. "Sounds fine. Thanks. I'll be ready."

"Saturday it is," he told her, turning away again. He climbed up into the cab and tried not to be too obvious about watching her walk back to her truck.

Something about the way a woman walked in a pair of jeans and boots, even ugly boots, made a man sit up and take notice. Like he hadn't noticed before this. To his disgust, he'd noticed when she'd worn a softball uniform and cleats. Not that it mattered. The woman was engaged to be married, after all, and on her way back to Dallas and her hotshot career as soon as her dad could do without her.

Sighing, Dean straightened his sunglasses as his son ran toward him, hauling the heavy water jug by its handle. He reached down a hand for the water jug as Donovan shoved it toward him. He stashed the jug in a corner then helped Donovan scramble up into the cab of the harvester before following him and settling into the operator's seat.

Donovan leaned against his back and said straight into his ear, "She sure is pretty, ain't she, Dad?"

He meant Ann, of course. Donovan had been playing pint-size matchmaker since Ann had literally caught him with his hand in the cookie jar. For the past year or more, since he'd come to understand what going to school really meant, Donovan had gone on the lookout for a mom. Dean figured it was as much concern about him being on his own during the time Donovan would be in school as it was the boy's natural desire for a mother. The boy didn't realize that most husbands and wives spent relatively little time together and that almost no fathers were blessed with the almost constant companionship of their children.

Dean mentally sorted through a number of possible replies, everything from correcting Donovan's grammar to playing dumb. In the end he chose casual honesty.

"She's pretty."

"And you like red hair, don'cha?"

"I do. But you realize that she doesn't actually live here, right?"

"Huh?"

"She's just visiting, son. Before long she'll go on back to where she came from and stay there."

"Huh. Is it a long ways off?"

"Yep. Afraid so."

Only a few hours away by car. Worlds away by every other measure.

But then that had always been the way with him and Ann Billings.

Donovan couldn't know that, of course.

Dean hoped that he never would.

Chapter Four

Jordan laughed when Ann told him about her boot-shopping experience, but not for the same reason that Dean had laughed.

"Why bother?" he asked during their phone conversation that evening. "You're only going to be there a few weeks. It's a foolish waste of money and time."

"You wouldn't say that if you could see the fields here. I can't wear my good shoes in this red dirt. They'll be ruined!"

"I suppose you have a point," Jordan grudgingly conceded. "I don't understand why the hired help can't handle things there, though. You have an important job here, and your family ought to realize that."

"Nothing is more important than my father's health, Jordan," she pointed out, "and the ranch hands work the livestock. They know little about the crops, especially now that Dad and Rex are moving into organic production."

"And what do you know about it?" he demanded.

"Only what I've been told," she admitted, "but someone has to give the orders, Jordan. I'm needed here. At least until Rex returns or Dad gets better. I thought you understood that."

He made a gusting sound. Then he said, "I guess I just miss you. We didn't have much time together before your brother's wedding pushed everything forward."

"The wedding didn't push things forward that much," she replied lightly before changing the subject. "Speaking of weddings, I've been thinking about a date for ours."

"Oh, I have, too," Jordan said briskly. "A date opened up here at the hotel for the last Saturday of July, and I think we should take it."

Ann bolted upright on the leather sofa in the living room of the ranch house. "The end of July! But that's…" She quickly did the mental math, torn between elation and panic. "That's eleven days away!"

"Eleven days and a year," he corrected, chortling. "Surely you didn't think I meant *this* year? You said you wanted a traditional wedding, after all. That takes time."

Ann blinked, feeling suddenly deflated. "Right.

Of course. How silly of me." She slumped back onto the sofa, frowning.

Her brother, Rex, and Callie had waited only a matter of days to marry. She'd thought their wedding a paltry thing compared to Rex's first one, but she couldn't deny that she'd never before seen the kind of joy on her brother's face that she saw when he looked at Callie. She knew that he regretted the failure of his first marriage, and she thanked God that he'd been given a second chance with Callie.

"There's always the possibility that the Copley-Mains wedding will be rescheduled and we'll have to pick another date," Jordan said. "I'm told that Samantha Copley changes her mind every other day."

"Oh," Ann mumbled. "Yes. I expect she'll change her mind in the middle of the ceremony."

"Well, we'll take the date anyway, and if she changes her mind again we'll adjust," he said lightly before changing the subject to business.

They spent the next hour talking about hotel issues before someone called Jordan away to handle something unexpected. Something unexpected was always coming up. That was why the manager lived on-site. Ann had tried to maintain a separate residence at first but had quickly realized the futility of it.

She went to bed that night feeling uneasy,

though she couldn't say why. She and Jordan were a good match. She loved him, and Jordan was eager to marry her. Wasn't he?

Of course he was! He'd made that abundantly clear. She smiled, telling herself that she was going to dream about her wedding.

Instead, she dreamed about a dog performing tricks and protecting a freckle-faced little redhead on command. And the tall, blond, blue-eyed trainer who so obviously devoted himself to that little redhead. She woke in the morning both dreading and looking forward to the shopping trip to come.

No doubt, Callie would have offered to make lunch for Dean and Donovan, but Ann hadn't had much experience in the kitchen. She could open a can, build a passable sandwich and operate the microwave, but she'd followed a recipe only a few times in her life, with mixed results. Meri was more domestic, having spent more time with their mother while Ann had hero-worshipped their older brother and done her best to compete with him.

Nine years her senior, Rex had always been patient with her—to a point, and Ann had always pushed to keep up with or even surpass her big brother. Only later did she realize how unattractive men found women who could and did compete with them. No matter how often she prayed that God would help her suppress her masculine traits, no matter how hard she tried to be more feminine, she just couldn't seem to overcome these undesirable tendencies. Still, she felt compelled to try.

Thankfully, Jordan seemed not to see that side of her. He knew her deepest, darkest secrets, and they didn't seem to matter to him. He valued her as a competent manager and organizer, and he obviously found no fault with her looks. They had much in common when it came to their careers and lifestyles. He'd seemed unconcerned when she'd told him that she wanted to wait till they were married to be together as man and wife, and had said that he wasn't currently a man of faith, but was open to Christianity, and promised that they could discuss it later when they had more time. She'd told herself that was a good sign.

Dean knew her from before, though. She already had a deficit to overcome with him. She couldn't risk spoiling lunch. So, after a longer than usual run and a light breakfast, she took her time dressing. She styled her hair with hot rollers and carefully applied makeup. She chose a pale floral lace tank top with skinny jeans and vanilla, leather spike heels. Once convinced that she appeared as feminine as possible for the task at hand, she went to the office and waited, going over the books and internet articles that Rex had left for her.

She heard footsteps on the porch at a few minutes past noon and was at the front door when the first knock sounded. Opening it the next instant, she greeted Dean with a smile. He wore a clean chambray shirt with the cuffs of his sleeves rolled back and the neck open. The blue heightened the gem-like color of his eyes, and the pale straw of his hat looked very much like the color of his blond hair. He was an amazingly attractive man, even in faded, dusty denim.

Next to him, Donovan wore a blue-and-green striped shirt, baggy jeans and a big smile. He looked up at her and proclaimed, "You look real pretty!"

Ann found that little-boy smile more and more difficult to resist. "Thank you, Donovan."

Dean looked her over and said, "Especially like the shoes."

She narrowed her eyes at him, pretending that she was not very much pleased. "They just aren't too good for tramping across fields."

"Exactly. I am extremely impressed that you can walk in them, though." He shot her a cheeky grin, flashing those dimples at her. "Ready to go?"

Rolling her eyes, she reached over and took

her small handbag from the half-moon foyer table. "I am now."

"Did you remember to bring socks?"

Socks. Of course. "Uh, one moment."

Turning, she hurried up to her room, where she snatched a pair of clean socks from the dresser. She had long ago gotten rid of sports and school memorabilia, leaving only the purple, tailored bed coverings and drapes. Before she left here this time, though, she was going to repaint this dresser and the shelving unit across the room. What had possessed her to paint all the drawer fronts and shelves different colors, anyway?

She rushed back downstairs, socks in hand. Dean and Donovan had stepped inside . "Thanks for reminding me," she said to Dean.

"Voice of experience," he told her, opening the front door.

She went out first, checking to be sure that she had the key before hitting the lock and pulling the door closed behind Dean, who followed Donovan. Her dad rarely locked the house, but her years in Dallas simply wouldn't allow her to walk away from an unlocked house. Dean's slight smile told her that he found the precaution unnecessary, but she would never forgive herself if she returned to find her dad's TVs and computer missing, not to mention her own electronic devices.

Of course, the horses and cattle could be taken by anyone bold enough to pull a trailer onto the place, though Wes had installed some motion detection devices at vulnerable spots along the fence line. He had an alarm panel set up in the office, and occasionally a coyote or bobcat set off one of the motion detectors. He'd warned her not to get upset if the alarm woke her, just to check the security screen, and if she saw nothing suspicious take a look at the recording in the morning. Rex, who was apparently some sort of expert on such things, had set up the recording component and arranged for cloud storage, but that security arrangement did not include the house, which seemed shortsighted to Ann.

She followed the Pryors to Dean's somewhat battered, white, double-cab, dually pickup truck. At least she supposed it was white under that thick layer of orange-red grime.

As if reading her thoughts, Dean said, "Hope you don't mind if we wash the truck before we head home." He opened the front passenger door with one hand and the backseat door with the other.

"We had to unload ever'thing so we could," Donovan informed her as he scrambled up into his car seat. "Gotta get out all the tools and stuff afore you can wash it."

Dean chuckled as he buckled Donovan into his seat. "Quite a job, isn't it, bud?" He glanced at Ann, who had yet to slip into her seat. "Donovan earned some extra money to buy school gear by helping me unload the truck bed this morning."

"I'm gonna get some cool stuff!" the boy exclaimed excitedly.

Ann smiled and stepped up into the surprisingly comfortable bucket seat. She was buckled before Dean slid in behind the steering wheel.

"War Bonnet Diner okay for lunch?"

"Is there any place else?"

"Not if you're hungry."

"I'm starved!" Donovan declared from his car seat in back.

"That makes two of us," Dean said, glancing into the rearview mirror as he pushed his sunglasses into place on his nose.

For a starving man, he didn't seem in much of a hurry. He drove in a leisurely fashion that had Ann setting her back teeth. In Dallas, where everyone was in a hurry all the time, he'd have been run off the road. The trip into War Bonnet covered fewer than six miles, but it seemed to take forever. They pulled into town, stopped at the blinking red light just past the Feed and

Grain on the edge of town, far longer than required to determine that no other vehicle could possibly impede their pathway, and rolled on.

Dean waved as they passed the gas station then tooted his horn at a madly grinning middle-aged woman in the grocery store parking lot.

"My aunt Deana," he explained.

Every other driver they passed waved or called out a greeting. War Bonnet boasted only a single city block of business buildings, including the town hall, bank, post office, a junk shop that billed itself as a collectibles store, a pair of empty spaces and the café. The school and athletic fields lay on the southwest side of town, beyond the four or five blocks of houses that comprised the remainder of War Bonnet, along with the small church on the southeast side. Her family had attended that church for most of her life, but her parents had switched to Countryside Church after she'd left home.

With tornadoes an ever-present danger in Oklahoma, the joke around War Bonnet was that a good-size dust devil could wipe it off the map. The little whirlwinds routinely whipped up red clouds of dust that danced down the streets, lashed the blooms off flowers, spattered windows with grit and stung eyes. One had even disconnected the electricity to the tornado siren near the school. After that the cable had been buried.

Dean found a parking space in front of one of the empty storefronts, and they walked up the sidewalk to the little café, which bustled with activity. The undisputed social center of the community, the café featured a long counter with eight stools, two booths in front of the plate-glass window and five tables, for a total capacity of thirty-six diners. Donovan begged to sit at the counter, but there were only two stools open, so Dean steered him toward a table in the back corner near a jukebox that hadn't worked in over a decade.

After escorting the boy to the bathroom to wash his hands, Dean ordered a hamburger and onion rings. Donovan asked for fish sticks and fries. Ann decided to try the fruit plate and chef's salad. It was better than she'd expected, but Dean's thick, fragrant hamburger made her mouth water. She'd forgotten how good a simple hamburger could smell. When Donovan offered to trade her fries for grapes, she gave him the grapes and declined the fries then accepted onion rings from Dean.

The moment she bit into the crisp ring, memories swept over her, fun times spent in this place with school friends and family. After she'd gotten her driver's license, she and her friends had hit this place after school, loading up on milk shakes, fries and onion rings before heading off to whatever commitments claimed them. She'd found such freedom in that. No more school buses to catch, no adults around to police their behavior—not that they'd misbehaved really. None of her group had drunk alcohol, used drugs or even dated much. They'd been too busy with school, sports, church, chores and getting their livestock ready for the county fair. True, they'd teased and gossiped and gotten loud, even broken out with the occasional short-lived food fight, but essentially they'd been harmless.

"Ann Billings," said a female voice, jolting her out of her reverie. Opening her eyes, Ann stared at the small, rounded, older woman. Something about her seemed familiar, but the short, curly, iron-gray hair and thick, owlish glasses brought no one to mind. Then the woman cupped her hands together and clucked her tongue, saying, "First your brother, now you. Will all the prodigals return to Straight Arrow Ranch?"

"Mrs. Lightner!"

The old dear smiled and held out her arms as Ann rose to her feet and bent forward for her hug. When she straightened again, she said to Dean and Donovan, "Mrs. Lightner was my Sunday School and piano teacher."

"Dean, Donovan," greeted the older woman,

nodding at each. "I'm surprised to see you all together."

"We're going shopping!" Donovan announced happily.

At the same time, Ann said, "Dean is doing some work for the ranch."

"I'm harvesting out at the Straight Arrow just now," Dean explained calmly. "And Donovan's ready to buy school supplies. Ann's going along to find a pair of boots."

"School supplies," Mrs. Lightner echoed. "First grade, is it?"

"Kindergarten," Dean corrected. "He turned five on Christmas Day."

"He's such a big boy that I thought he must be six at least," Mrs. Lightner said. She turned her full attention on Donovan, saying, "You'll do very well, I'm sure."

Donovan nodded eagerly. "Yes, ma'am." He frowned then. "But how come they won't let me take my dog?"

"I'll need Digger with me," Dean told him.

"Oh, that's true," Mrs. Lightner confirmed, nodding sagely. "Even though it's just half a day, your dad will miss you. He'll need the dog to keep him company. You'll have lots of new friends and teachers, but Dad will be missing his right-hand man."

Donovan sighed. Then he abruptly brightened, split a look between Ann and his father and shook a finger in Dean's face, proclaiming, "You need to get a wife."

"Whoa!" Dean cried, shoving back his chair.

"Out of the mouths of babes," Mrs. Lightner chortled.

"Your grandma can shake a finger at me, buddy, but you cannot," Dean scolded lightly, crumpling his napkin and dropping it beside his plate. "Now, let's get this show on the road. I have things to do today."

Donovan crammed the last bit of fish into his mouth, rubbed a paper napkin over his face and slid down off his chair. Ann stood as Dean pulled his wallet from his pocket and tossed several bills onto the table.

"You're driving, so let me pay for lunch," she said quickly, hoping that would squelch any suppositions that Mrs. Lightner might have about the two of them dating.

He looked at her, his face blank, shrugged and slid his wallet back into his pocket, leaving the gratuity on the table. "Suits me."

Relieved, Ann reached for her purse. At the same time, she felt an unexpected and puzzling sense of disappointment. She didn't have time to think about it, though, as Mrs. Lightner surprised her by sliding her arm through Ann's.

"How is your father?" the older woman asked.

"He's in the city with Meredith for chemo-therapy," Ann told her. "Meri calls every day. It sounds pretty tough, but we're trusting that he'll come through okay."

"Everyone here at the town church is praying for him," Mrs. Lightner said.

"Thank you," Ann replied. "We appreciate that."

"So how long are you going to stay?" Mrs. Lightner asked, walking with her to the cash register.

"As long as I'm needed. At least until Rex and Callie get matters settled in Tulsa and come home. My fiancé is filling in for me with my job," Ann said pointedly.

"You're engaged?"

"That's right. If you were at the wedding, you probably saw him."

"I did attend the wedding but not the reception," Mrs. Lightner mused, obviously thinking. She looked up suddenly. "Distinguished, older man, graying temples, expensive suit?"

Older man? Graying temples? Ann would have said silver, not gray, but the expensive suit nailed it. She put on a smile. "That's right."

Mrs. Lightner looked to Dean, who waited by the door with Donovan. "Well," she said, "to each her own." Then she hugged Ann again, said her farewells and left.

Stung for reasons that she couldn't quite explain, Ann waved over the waitress, paid the bill and followed the Pryors out onto the sidewalk. She watched them strolling along in front of her, Dean's large, capable hand resting against his son's narrow back while Donovan talked excitedly about some subject that escaped her. Then again, Donovan never seemed to speak in any other fashion. He was an excited, happy, obviously well-loved little boy. And apparently something of a matchmaker.

She wondered where his mother was, then she realized that she'd been trying very hard *not* to wonder. Donovan had told her, of course, that he didn't have a mom, that his grandmother did his laundry, but Ann purposefully hadn't pursued the subject because she really hadn't wanted to know. Knowing the situation would somehow open her to…speculations, unwelcome, unnecessary, troublesome speculations of the sort that no engaged woman should entertain. Especially a woman as unsuited to being a mother as Ann thought herself to be.

Standing aside, she waited while Dean belted Donovan into his safety seat. Then, to her surprise, Dean walked straight past her on his way around the truck. She knew instantly that she'd somehow insulted him, probably by insisting on paying for lunch.

"Dean."

He halted at the front of the truck and reached out a hand to thump a thumb against the hood, but he didn't turn or speak.

"I didn't mean to upset you."

He turned his head then, that cold, blank look on his face. "What makes you think I'm upset?"

"I don't know. I—I just thought it was fair that I pay for lunch."

Nodding, he looked away. "Uh-huh. I really didn't expect anything else from you, Jolly." With that, he walked around the truck and opened the driver's door. He stood there, waiting, until she opened the passenger door and got into the truck.

She didn't know what to say or think, and she really couldn't get into it with Donovan sitting there in the backseat. As it was, the boy sensed the tension.

"Everything okay?" he asked, leaning forward.

Dean turned a warm smile over his shoulder even as he reached for the ignition switch. "Sure, bud. What could be wrong?"

Apparently satisfied, Donovan sat back and began enumerating the items he intended to buy. Ann smiled and nodded.

Like Dean said, what could be wrong?

Or was she avoiding the more important questions? Like, why couldn't she escape the feeling that something very important was wrong?

Why did it suddenly feel as if her whole life was wrong?

Chapter Five

❧

"Look at this, Dad!"

Donovan held up a red plastic container in the shape of a car with real wheels. Decals depicted the windows and other details, but it could be rolled.

"It's a pencil case," Dean explained, opening the thing to expose the sharpener and storage compartments.

"Cool! Can I get it?"

Dean pulled out his phone and activated the calculator function. "Well, it's not on the list, but let's see if it's in your budget." He helped the boy find the price, figure the tax and deduct the amount from his available funds. Next they checked to make sure the pencil case would fit in Donovan's chosen backpack. "Looks like you'd still have enough to finish your list, so if this is the bonus item you'd like to choose, you can get it."

Crowing, the boy spun around on the heel of his shoe. The pencil box functioned in several ways, one of them being a toy, all for under five dollars. Donovan couldn't have been happier. Ann couldn't have been more impressed. Whatever else he might be, Dean Paul Pryor was a great father. Dean had clearly taught his son the value of a dollar, how to shop and prioritize and to be happy with the most functional things. Later, when they moved on to clothing, she found herself seeking his guidance for her own purchases.

"What do you think of these boots?"

"Real good-looking," he answered, turning one over in his hands. "I'd buy them myself if I could afford them. For Sunday best."

"Not for every day?"

He shook his head, set down the ostrich leather boot and reached for another, one with a rounder toe, lower heel, wider vamp and crepe sole. He tossed it in his hand, saying, "This boot here is lighter by several ounces, easier to get on and off, far better padded where it counts most and it's got a steel toe." She looked down to see a much more scuffed boot in a different leather finish on his own foot.

"Mine's roughout," he said. "You can get this

same style in a true suede or a slick leather, even exotics, though I don't recommend that."

She reached for a slick leather in a medium reddish-brown.

"You'll have to polish that one to keep it looking good," he pointed out, "but it's a better-looking boot, for sure."

"I don't mind a little polishing," she said, turning the boot over in her hand.

He smiled. "Try it on."

She quickly discovered what he meant about padding where it counted most—and that her skinny jeans looked a little odd tucked into the tops of these boots, which were not as tall as the showy pair she'd bought in Duncan. She decided to let Dean advise her on the proper cut of jeans to go with her new boots.

The new jeans felt strangely familiar when she slipped them on, and she couldn't help smiling when she recalled wearing Rex's old hand-me-downs. How simple and carefree life had seemed back then. Secure in the love and acceptance of her family, all she'd cared about was the day's activities. She'd never even stopped to wonder what anyone else thought of her. Frowning, she suddenly worried that she might be slipping back into harmful old habits.

When she stepped out of the dressing room,

however, Dean's eyes lit up with unmistakable approval. Still, she couldn't help feeling concern.

Twisting at the waist, she asked, "You don't think they're too masculine?"

He barked laughter. "On you? You're the girl who rocked a pair of cleats and a batting helmet. Now you're worried about looking masculine?"

Was he saying that she'd looked good in cleats and a helmet or that it was too late to worry about her femininity? At least Donovan's opinion seemed unambiguous.

"She looks pretty, don't she, Dad?"

Dean ruffled the boy's shaggy hair, saying, "Of course."

Still doubtful, Ann turned her back to the mirror and looked over her shoulder in time to catch Dean's expression in the mirror.

Rolling his eyes, he said, "Look, who's going to see you, anyway? It's not like you'll wear these things anywhere but the field. Right?"

That was true. No one but the ranch hands and these two would likely see her dressed like this. It was far too late to try to impress Dean, and the ranch hands still thought of her as that little girl who ran around the place in her brother's outgrown clothes, so what did she have to lose?

"I'll take them," she decided, and just for old times' sake she'd take a couple of lightweight, long-sleeved shirts, too. If nothing else, they'd help keep the freckles on her arms at bay. She'd leave them here when she returned to Dallas, and Jordan would never be the wiser. Meanwhile, she'd at least be more comfortable while on the job at Straight Arrow Ranch. And maybe—just maybe—she'd feel some of that old, carefree joy, too.

The snoring from the backseat made Dean chuckle. He had no doubt that they'd worn out the boy. Donovan had been dragging his steps long before they'd gotten back to the truck. He'd been snoring almost before his belt had been buckled on his safety seat. Dean knew his son well, though, and he wasn't buying it.

After nearly an hour of silence, as soon as Dean turned the dually onto Straight Arrow Road, Ann asked, "Dean, what did you mean earlier when you said that you didn't expect anything else from me?"

He'd suspected that she'd been stewing about that, but he still hadn't decided exactly how to answer her. He wouldn't be giving her an explanation in front of his son, though. Lifting a finger to his lips, he brought the truck to a safe stop beside the house and shifted around in his seat.

"Hey, pard," he said quietly, "I'm going to walk Miss Ann to her door now. Okay?"

Donovan's eyes popped open. He sat up straight and grinned. "Sure."

Dean looked at Ann, who bowed her head to hide her smile. "You wait right here. I won't be long."

"I'm real tired," the boy said, sounding anything but. "I'll just take another nap."

"You do that," Dean replied, glancing pointedly at Ann again before opening his door and stepping out of the truck, leaving his hat behind.

She let herself out before he could gather up her packages from the backseat and get around to do it, but he supposed that was to be expected considering how he'd acted earlier. He felt a certain amount of shame about that now. He'd had no right to feel slighted by her before; she just seemed to have that effect on him sometimes; too often, actually. Catching up to her, he walked alongside her, his arms laden with bags and boxes, until they were well beneath the trees on the pathway to the porch.

"Let's face it," he finally said, "Donovan was matchmaking back there at the diner, and it made you uncomfortable. I expected you to show Mrs. Lightner that he's barking up the wrong tree, and you did just that."

"So he's done this before," Ann mused.

"Uh, not really," Dean had to say. "It's not like single women are thick on the ground around here. My grandma's always urging me to get out and date, and it's obvious that he *wants* a mother. I—I think it's a matter of you showing up at the right time, and that hair."

"Just as he's about to start school, you mean."

"Exactly."

She reached up and touched her head. "The hair, though…"

They stepped onto the porch.

"*He* has red hair. *You* have red hair," Dean explained. "To him that means you look like his mother. Makes you a prime candidate."

"Ah."

"Of course, I know you're not interested in us." Even though he'd had a terrible crush on her as a boy. She hadn't known it, still didn't know it, and he had no intention of informing her, no more than he had of explaining that her eagerness to rid Mrs. Lightner of any hint that they might be dating, or were even friends, had unexpectedly hurt him.

"Look, Dean," Ann began, but just then the front door opened, and her sister, Meredith, stepped out. "Meri!" Ann exclaimed. "I wasn't expecting you until tomorrow."

"Dad couldn't wait another day to get home. He's terribly ill, though, Annie. I had to pull the car right up to the back door to get him into the house." That probably explained why Dean hadn't spotted the vehicle when he'd driven in, that and Ann's question.

"Oh, honey, I'm sorry I wasn't here when you arrived," Ann was saying. "I wish you'd let me know you were coming."

"I meant to, but frankly I had my hands full just getting him here." Meredith glanced at Dean then, adding, "Looks like you've got your hands full, too." He stepped forward as she reached out and began shifting his burdens to her and Ann, while she explained they'd been shopping.

"Thanks so much for your help with this, Dean."

"My pleasure," he told Ann. "Please let Wes know that Grandma and I are praying for him."

"That means a lot," Meredith said.

"Don't hesitate to call on us if we can do anything else."

Nodding, Ann said, "Say goodbye to Donovan for me."

"Absolutely."

He walked away heavy of heart. Wes Billings was a good man, and Dean hoped fervently that he would beat this awful disease, for Wes's sake but also for the sakes of his children and everyone who knew them. He sensed instinctively that if Wes didn't make it, Ann would likely never step foot in War Bonnet again. Something about that struck Dean as deeply, desperately, sadly wrong.

* * *

To Dean's surprise, Ann showed up at Countryside Church the next morning. He'd assumed that her father's illness would keep her away. She'd grown up in this area, so folks greeted her warmly, not that they wouldn't have done the same for a stranger, but she was Wes Billings's girl, and that meant something around here. It didn't hurt that she looked like a peacock among hens in a shiny, cornflower-blue suit that ignited her eyes and made her skin glow. The slim skirt and high heels accentuated her height and long legs. How she walked in them he would never know, but he liked that she didn't try to hide her height. So many tall women did, and it just made them look uncertain and awkward. Ann Billings looked ready to take on the world and left the impression that she could do it without breaking a fingernail.

Still, she looked a little sad and lonely sitting all alone. If Donovan had been there instead of children's church, he'd have rushed up and thrown his arms around her. Dean didn't have his son's confidence that his greeting would be returned with equal warmth, so he contented himself with a nod and a mumble.

"Nice to see you."

His grandmother scolded him, in her fashion, after the service.

"You need to speak to her, Dean. You've had more to do with her than anyone here, I figure, and the Billingses have been good to us."

Betty Gladys Pryor was a stout, tall woman who wore her long, gray hair curled into a droopy bun on the back of her head and gave up her jeans and T-shirts for a dress only on Sundays, but Dean had never known her to own a pair of nylon stockings or a tube of lipstick. She'd worked alongside her husband in the field when they'd farmed wheat and raised two daughters, one of whom—Dean's mother, Wynona—had been a terrible disappointment. Betty still managed a good acre of a vegetable garden every year, as well as her grandson and great-grandson. She spoke her mind but never with rancor and faced each day with calm, patient acceptance and the expectation of joy. Dean had learned, with some difficulty, to value her advice and opinions, but if she had a failing it was thinking more highly of him than she had any reason to.

"Don't you go getting any ideas," he grumbled, even as he began to forge a path through the disbanding crowd to Ann's side. Betty snagged a forefinger in his belt loop and tagged along in his wake.

"How's your dad doing?" Dean asked as soon as he reached Ann, who had yet to leave her pew because of the people gathered around her. She turned a smile on him and spoke in a voice loud enough for all to hear.

"It's pretty rough right now. He isn't allowed many visitors for fear of infection while his immune system is at a low ebb, but Meredith is taking good care of him. He wanted me here today specifically to let y'all know that he appreciates your prayers and support."

"Anything we can do?" someone asked.

"Mostly keep up those prayers," Ann answered.

"You sure got those," someone else said.

"A card now and again would brighten his day," she suggested.

"We can make that happen," one of the women said, and she stepped away with two or three others to discuss a mail campaign.

The crowd began to break up. His grandmother edged forward then, and Dean introduced her.

"Ann, I'm not sure you've ever met my grandmother. Grandma, this is Ann Billings. Ann, my grandmother, Betty Pryor."

"So nice to meet you, Mrs. Pryor."

"Oh, call me Betty or Grandma. Everyone does. Forgive me if I'm stepping on your toes, sugar, but with Callie away, your sister nursing your dad and you running things up at the

Straight Arrow, I'm wondering if you couldn't use some good old-fashioned home cooking about now. I'm no Gloria Billings, but I can put together a meat loaf right quick. What do you say?"

Ann looked to Dean, and he could see the relief in her eyes but also the polite protest she was forming. He spoke before she could.

"You put it together, Grandma. I'll deliver it."

Ann gave in without a fight. "Thank you so much. Callie put up what she could for us, but I'm not even any good at reheating it. I always get the oven too hot or the burner too high. And Meri has her hands full right now. If Dad could just get one decent meal…"

"Tell you what," Grandma said, taking Ann's hand. "I've got some chicken soup canned for when Donovan gets his usual winter croup. I'll send that over, too, and a few other things that are still sitting around from last year's garden. Maybe some creamed corn or bean soup would ease Wes's stomach. You can warm that in the microwave."

"Mrs. Pry—Betty, you are a Godsend," Ann declared.

Just then, Donovan came barreling through a side door. "Dad!"

His teacher waved at Dean to let him know

that she hadn't just turned the boy loose. "Sorry!" Dean called. "Got a little held up."

"Donovan, please don't run or shout in the sanctuary," Dean instructed as the boy crashed into his side, waving his class papers.

"Yessir. Boy, we had a good story. Did you know about Lazarus?"

"I did."

"He died, and it was so long he was probably all stinky and everything, but Jesus brought him back." Before Dean could even remark on that, Donovan turned to his great-grandmother. Then he spied Ann and threw himself at her, nearly knocking her backward in his exuberance.

She laughed, staggering behind his hug. "Hello to you, too."

Donovan promptly backed up a step, tilted back his head and declared, "Wow, you sure are pretty."

Ann glanced around uncertainly, but then she smiled and said, "Why, thank you, Donovan."

He grabbed his father's hand and said to Betty. "She sure is pretty, ain't she, Grandma?"

"*Isn't* she," Dean corrected, trying not to look at Ann as he said it.

Grandma hid her smile behind her hand and nodded before answering. "She sure is. That color suits her very well."

Ann shook her head, blushing.

"Come on, you," Dean said, rescuing her by grasping Donovan's shoulders and turning him up the aisle. "We have to get going. Grandma has some cooking to do."

"Woo-hoo!" Donovan crowed.

"What did I say about shouting in the sanctuary?" Dean reminded him.

Ducking his head, Donovan lowered his voice to a near-whisper. "Woo-hoo." Dean started him toward the doors at the back of the long room. "I'm hungry enough to eat a horse," Donovan claimed to no one in particular, "A dead, stinky horse."

Behind them, Grandma and Ann laughed. Dean liked the sound of their mingled voices, and—not for the first time—he wished that he could be as free with his compliments as his son was with his. That ring on Ann's finger tied Dean's tongue, though, not that she wanted to hear compliments from him in any event, a fact he would do well to remember in the future.

By the time Ann heard tires on the red dirt road outside the ranch house later that afternoon, she was half out of her mind.

"That has to be Dean."

"Whoever it is, get them in here," Meredith barked, holding their father's head as he slumped into the corner by the bathroom door.

"You should've called me," she scolded for perhaps the tenth time as Ann ran for the front door.

"Man's...got his...pride," Wes gasped.

Ann was still shaking her head about that when she opened the front door to find Dean ambling along the path toward the porch, a big cardboard box in his arms.

"Hurry!" she exclaimed. "We need your help."

He broke into long, loping strides. She stepped back, holding open both the screen and the front doors.

"What's wrong?" he asked as he slipped past her, the box clutched to his chest.

"Dad fell on his way back from the bathroom, and we can't get him up."

"Where is he?"

She hurried around him and quickly led the way through the foyer and along the hallway past the living room and back staircase into the spacious kitchen, where he left the box and his hat on the table. They rushed across the room and into the back hallway to the first door on the left.

Rex had brought in a hospital bed and opened a doorway into an updated bath behind the mudroom so their dad could make a convenient downstairs bed suite in the space their mom had once claimed for her crafts and sewing. The room was large enough to allow for a dresser and a couple comfortable chairs, a flat-screen television and bedside tables, and the wheelchair that Wes so hated to use. Ann and her sister had done their best to dress up the space with fresh paint, their late mother's needlework and filmy curtains on the large windows overlooking the side yard. The hardwood floors were clean, bare and even.

Meredith popped up from the far side of the bed by the bathroom door.

"Oh, thank God you're here, Dean. We can't lift him."

Dean shot across the room and rounded the bed, going down on his haunches next to Wes, who lay crumpled into the corner.

"You okay there, Wes? Did you hit your head?"

"I think he knocked his elbow against the wall, but he doesn't seem to have broken anything," Meredith answered.

"Pushed it…a little…too far," Wes panted, lifting an arm toward Dean.

Gingerly looping Wes's arm around his neck, Dean scooped his own arms around Wes's shoulders and hips, asking, "Do you think you can get your feet under you?"

"Think so," Wes muttered, wrapping his other arm around Dean.

"Okay. Let's get you up."

Standing, Dean literally lifted Wes with him.

He scrabbled for a moment, but then Wes got his feet planted and stiffened his legs. Ann noted that as soon as Wes was standing, Dean shifted, keeping a supportive arm about her dad. Obviously Dean was doing his best to afford her father every dignity. Ann felt tears fill her eyes and quickly busied herself straightening the covers on her dad's bed. Wes sidled closer and eased himself down onto the edge of the bed, Dean supporting him all the way.

As soon as Dean backed away, Meredith stepped in and removed the slippers from their father's feet, lifting his legs up and onto the bed and making him comfortable.

"How's your stomach?"

Wes laid a large, bony hand across his flat middle. Despite the thirty pounds or more he'd dropped in the past weeks, he was still a big man, but the chemo had taken his once lush, cinnamon-and-sugar hair, giving him a cadaverish look that broke Ann's heart every time she saw him.

"Pretty rumbly."

Meredith plunked a basin down on the bed beside him, saying sternly, "No arguments. I don't want you getting out of this bed without help again. I've seen lots of men throwing up, you know."

"Not your father," Wes grumbled.

"Dad, that's what I'm here for," Meredith pointed out. "And I *am* a nurse, you know."

Sighing, he nodded. "I know."

Briskly, she set about filling a syringe from a tray on the bedside table. "I'm going to give you an injection now to settle your stomach. Then I want you to eat something before the medication knocks you out. All right?"

"Grandma sent over some jars of chicken soup," Dean said helpfully.

"I'll heat some up," Meredith volunteered, lifting the sleeve of Wes's T-shirt and wiping his skin with an alcohol swab before injecting him with the medication.

"Maybe Dean…will stay…and help me to the table," Wes said.

"Be happy to," Dean replied at once.

"You can eat on a tray here," Meredith argued, but Wes gave her a hard look.

"Table," he insisted.

Meredith rolled her eyes and pointed at the wheelchair. "As long as you use that."

Wes sighed. "Fine."

Meredith quickly finished up and left the room. Ann didn't feel that she should leave their guest, especially after he'd helped them.

"Betty sent some other things, as well, Dad," Ann said, nodding at a chair for Dean. He walked around the bed and sat down.

She perched on the side of her father's bed and smiled at Dean as Wes said, "Good of her."

"She's glad to do it," Dean told him. "Anything we can do to help." Wes put out his hand and Dean took it, saying, "Maybe you'd like to pray before your meal gets here."

"Please," Wes replied, closing his eyes.

Dean braced his elbows on his knees, Wes's hand clasped in both of his, and began to pray, quietly, calmly, competently.

Ann noticed that Dean's hands very much resembled her father's. Both were square-palmed and long-fingered, large and capable. These were the hands of working men, men who used their backs as well as their brains, strong, masculine, sure of their purposes and their abilities.

Suddenly she thought of Jordan's soft, well-manicured hands, and a shiver ran through her, something that felt terribly like revulsion. But that couldn't be right.

She loved Jordan.

Didn't she?

Chapter Six

By the time Meredith had their father's lunch ready, Wes's stomach seemed settled and his strength somewhat restored. He didn't complain when Dean helped him into the wheelchair, and he managed to eat a fair-sized bowl of Betty's rich chicken soup with some hot bread that Meredith came up with from somewhere. His eyelids drooping, he began to nod off even before Ann had served up plates of meat loaf and green beans for herself, Meri and Dean, even though Dean protested that he'd already eaten a sandwich before coming over.

Wes insisted on staying at the table until Dean had finished his own meal. Ann had never seen a man make food disappear so fast—or been so grateful for it. He was wheeling her dad back into his room within minutes. Ann went with them and watched gratefully the careful, respectful manner in which Dean shifted Wes back into the bed, allowing him to do as much for himself as possible. She didn't have Meri's gift for caring, but Ann did her best to make her dad comfortable, kissed his cheek and left him drifting into slumber after hearing Dean promise to come again.

They returned to the kitchen to find that Meredith had dished up some ice cream for Dean. Chuckling, Dean sat down to the table again.

"You Billings women act like Grandma doesn't feed me," he joked, lifting his spoon.

"We just want to thank you for your help today," Meredith said, smiling at Ann.

She and Meredith finished their lunch while he polished off his ice cream. Then Ann walked him to the front door, Meredith calling out her thanks to his grandmother for the food.

"She'll be pleased to have been of service," Dean told her.

"I don't know what we'd have done without you," Ann began when they reached the front door, suddenly choking up. She could usually put her dad's illness out of mind and carry on, but today it had hit her especially hard, and she felt tears fill her eyes again.

"Mind a bit of advice?" Dean asked.

She shook her head, knuckling moisture from

her eyes. "Seems like I'm always coming to you for advice."

"Don't let him see you cry. When my grandfather was ill, what worried him, what hurt him most, was seeing my grandmother's grief and fear. I realized that the best thing I could do for him was to hide my tears and allow him as much dignity as possible. Wasting away is hard on a proud, strong man."

Before she knew it, tears streamed down her face, and she couldn't stop them. She realized that she'd instinctively been holding them back, and now she knew why.

"Here now," Dean said softly, pulling her into his arms. "I shouldn't have said anything. Wes isn't wasting away. He's fighting. This isn't the same at all."

"It is," she whispered against his shoulder.

"No, no. Grandpa had lots more against him than cancer. He had a bad heart, and he couldn't put down the cigarettes. His lung cancer was too far gone when they found it, and that was ten years ago. They've improved treatment since then."

"You're right, though," she said through her tears. "We've been trying to baby him, and no father wants to appear weak in front of his daughters. On some level I knew, but…he's my dad." Her voice thinned and broke on the last word.

Dean's big hand cupped the back of her head and his strong arms just held her as she struggled to pull herself together.

"It's okay," he crooned. "Wes is going to be okay."

"I know," she managed after a long, tearful moment. "I believe that. I really do. It's just hard to see him this way."

"I understand."

She nodded, sniffed back the last of her tears and began to pull away. "I'm sure you do."

After a moment's hesitation, Dean loosened his embrace and shifted back. "Better now?"

Smiling, she wiped her face with her fingertips. "Yes. Thank you."

"No problem."

She finally met his gaze. "No, seriously. Thank you for everything."

He lifted his hand and gently cradled her cheek. "Anytime, Jolly. Anytime at all." Dropping his hand, he briskly added, "See you tomorrow."

Briefly touching the wet spot on his shoulder, she nodded. "Yes. Tomorrow." Chuckling, he turned and opened the door. "Say hello to Donovan for me."

"Promise." He went off with a wave, fitting his hat to his head.

Ann reluctantly closed the door and leaned her shoulder against it, wondering what was happening here. Just a few days ago, she'd felt nothing but disdain for Dean Paul Pryor. Now...now she felt a warm gratitude, a great respect and a good deal of liking.

She looked at the ring on her finger and frowned. More liking than seemed wise. She didn't even mind when he called her Jolly anymore.

Troubled by her thoughts and feelings, Ann found a few minutes, later that afternoon, to call Jordan. He answered the phone after only a few rings, which told her that he wasn't especially busy. At times he had to let calls go to voice mail and get back to her when he wasn't dealing with hotel issues. She felt a good deal of relief at the sound of his voice.

"Well, hello there, Oklahoma. I was just thinking of you."

"That's nice to know," she told him, "especially after the day I've had."

"Rough going?"

"Dad's very sick. I guess it's to be expected, but it's really hard to watch."

"How long do you think he has?"

Stunned by the casual manner in which Jordan

had tossed the question out there, Ann gasped. Then she got angry.

"Jordan! How dare you say such a thing? He's not dying."

"You said—"

"He's going to beat this, Jordan. He's fighting, and he's going to beat this."

"Of course he is," Jordan said soothingly. "I didn't mean that the way it sounded. It's just that I miss you and can't help but wonder how long we're going to be apart. That's all I meant."

But was it? And why didn't Jordan's reassurance comfort her as much as Dean's had?

She told herself that it was all about proximity. Dean was here; Jordan was a hundred and fifty miles away. Dean could see what was happening with her father. Jordan's reality was the hotel and its myriad problems and details. He had only secondhand information about what went on at the ranch, so how could she expect him to understand her fear and pain?

The vision of Dean sitting at her father's bedside quietly praying came to her, and she knew that Jordan would not even begin to do such a thing. He'd likely be horrified if asked to. Not so long ago, that idea wouldn't have bothered her a great deal.

Now, somehow, it did. Very much.

* * *

Once he started praying, Dean couldn't seem to stop. He'd only been fifteen when his grandfather had died, but he remembered those dark days all too well. The shock of learning of his grandfather's illness still reverberated through him whenever he thought of it. Within a very few months—weeks, really—a seemingly strong, almost invincible, man had weakened, shriveled, faded and quickly passed from this life to the next. The family hadn't even had time to adjust to the idea of his illness before he was gone.

Dean didn't want to see that happen to Ann and her family. He hated the very thought of Wes's suffering, and Ann's tears made him want to storm Heaven's gates on their behalf. After leaving the Straight Arrow, he tried to turn his mind from their situation, but the feel of Ann in his arms, the dampness of his shirt, the cracking of her voice all weighed on his mind. Yet, what could he do other than pray?

He did so silently and often throughout the rest of the afternoon and evening, and Grandma somehow knew it. She came to him as soon as Donovan was tucked up in his bed for the night.

Dean sat on the stoop in the corner of the porch that wrapped around the front of the two-story, white-clapboard, T-shaped house. Grandma dropped down beside him, pulled her knees up and hugged them. She didn't beat around the bush.

"How bad is Wes?"

Dean shrugged. "I don't know. He looks bad. No hair, pale, thin. But I can't say whether he's going to make it or not. The chemo is obviously pretty rough, but I doubt even the doctors know what the real status of the disease is yet."

"Well, treatment has improved a lot."

"That's what I told Ann."

Several telling heartbeats later, Grandma asked oh-so-casually, "How is she?"

Dean tried to sound just as casual. "Worried. Broken up. She tries to keep it together in front of him, but she and Meredith both need to back off a bit and let him do what he can for himself."

"I don't suppose you told her that." Dean shrugged, and Betty patted him on the knee. "You did tell her that. Well, don't take it so hard. She'll think about it and realize you were trying to help."

"No, it's not like that," he said. "It's just that I upset her, made her cry. I brought up Grandpa and scared her."

"Hmm." Grandma touched the faint stain on his shirt. "Cried on your shoulder, did she?"

"Now, don't make more of it than there is," Dean warned. "Her dad's ill. She was upset."

"Uh-huh."

"*And* she's engaged."

"Engaged isn't married," Grandma said, getting up to go inside. "Just saying."

"And I'm just saying that you're being silly," Dean told her as she walked across the porch.

"Well, if I'm silly, we can both laugh about it later," she drawled. "Good night, hon."

"Night," Dean muttered as she went inside.

She *was* being silly, Dean told himself, very silly. And so was he.

Once he'd had Ann in his arms today, he hadn't wanted to let her go. He'd wanted to sweep her up, carry her off and promise to make everything okay. He'd wanted to kiss away her tears and return that saucy, bring-on-the-world smile to her face. He'd wanted…all sorts of things to which he had no right and for which he had no hope.

And so he prayed. For Ann. For her dad. And for himself.

In the end, he decided that the best thing he could do was keep his distance from Ann Billings. It wouldn't be easy, given the situation, but it would be wise. So that, ultimately, became his prayer.

Lord, make me wise.

By the time Ann arrived in the field on Monday morning, Dean was already hard at work.

She waved, and he waved back but didn't stop the combine or try to speak to her. Donovan ran up, his dog on his heels, to give her one of his body-blow hugs and a smile as wide as his face. Seeing that he was essentially alone in the field while his father worked, she offered to take the boy back to the house with her, but he claimed that his dad "needed" him to watch the water cooler that sat on the open tailgate of the truck until he was "needed" in the cab of the combine.

Ann had to admire Dean's parenting skills. He kept the boy close and taught him responsibility by giving him small jobs that he could perform while playing. One day Donovan would realize those jobs were imaginary, but hopefully by then he'd also realize how deeply and skillfully his father cared for him.

She let the happy boy show her how Digger drank from the stream of water that fell from the spigot of the cooler when he turned it on, then she left him to scamper around with his dog until Dean took him up into the cab of the harvester. No doubt Donovan would grow bored shut up inside the cab of the harvester all day. This way, Dean broke up the monotony for him while keeping him within sight and allowing him a certain freedom.

Only as she drove back to the house did she wonder if Dean might be avoiding her, but she had no real reason to think that. Telling herself that she couldn't trust her feelings just now, she pushed aside the suspicion and focused on what needed to be done. Fearing that she was becoming too fond of Dean, she didn't go out to the field the next day. After all, if she couldn't trust him to do what needed to be done by now, she'd know it already. On Wednesday morning Dean called to say that he'd finish the oat harvest and would be delivering the fodder to the appropriate new storage bins later that afternoon.

Wes felt well enough to watch from the living room window as Ann went out to oversee the delivery. She hadn't expected Dean to have extra hands with him, but the oats arrived in a pair of two-and-a-half-ton trucks. Dean, Donovan and the dog rode in the first; two other men came in the second. Well past trying to impress Dean, Ann had dressed simply in a lightweight, long-sleeved top, tied at her waist, work jeans and her new, plain boots. With her hair caught in a ponytail low on the back of her head, she'd crammed her old baseball cap onto her head before going out to wait for them.

Dean got the first truck into position, and the men were hauling out a huge vacuum hose to siphon the oats from the truck bed into the storage tank when Donovan and the dog came to greet her. As usual, Donovan nearly knocked her over with his hug. Laughing, she bent and scooped him up against her before setting him down again, Digger barking and scampering around them happily. The kid was surprisingly heavy, a solid hunk of boy. Dean left the truck and walked over to them, smiling.

"Well, look at you," he said, stripping off his sunglasses. "You've turned into the best-looking ranch hand I've ever seen."

As soon as he said it, he ducked his head, as if embarrassed, but Ann had never felt so flattered. Glancing around, she muttered thanks and caught the other men sneaking looks at her. Suddenly feeling a bit self-conscious, she turned and moved a little distance off. After a moment Dean followed, sliding his glasses back onto his face.

"Everything go all right?" she asked casually.

"It's a good harvest. Oats are in excellent shape. Wes should be pleased."

Ann nodded. "I'll tell him."

"We'll get started on the mixing station in the morning. Once the sorghum is in, you'll be able to mix your feeds right here."

"I'll make sure Dad and Rex know where we are with the schedule. I assume you'll be wanting a check now."

"It can wait until tomorrow. I won't pay these men until then."

"All right."

He stepped off, waving for her to follow and slapping his billed cap onto his head. "If you want to come over here, I'll show you where the mixer will stand."

"Sure."

Rex had given her a good idea about it all, but Dean explained in detail. The whole thing made perfect sense now that she fully understood. Suddenly the dowdy, dusty old ranch where she had grown up was starting to feel like a thriving, modern business, not that it had ever been failing. Her dad had kept the ranch in decent shape financially, but she knew that he had worries now that the medical bills were stacking up. Even with insurance, the bills came in with dismaying regularity. With Rex pumping new investment and energy into the place, though, she didn't doubt that the Straight Arrow Ranch would quickly be more prosperous than ever. Ann sensed that her dad was eager to get out here and be part of it all again; she prayed that would soon be the case.

Dean apparently felt the same undercurrents. He glanced around, smiling, and lifted his shoulders. "It's kind of exciting, what's going on around here."

"I think so."

He seemed surprised by that. "Really?"

"Well, sure. Dad and Rex have big plans for this place."

Turning a slow circle to take a good look around, Dean said, "I wish them every success." Coming to a stop, he looked down at her, a wry smile curving his lips. "And frankly I wish I had their vision and business acumen."

"What makes you think you don't?"

"Oh, the fact that I work sunup to sundown and just barely manage to get by," he said lightly.

"You're raising a son on your own," she pointed out, "and you've got a lot of skills."

"Maybe so, but I haven't figured out how to best make them work for me yet," he said with a wry smile. "But I will. Eventually." One of the men called to him, and he lifted his chin in acknowledgement. "Gotta switch the trucks."

"I'll leave you to it." She began backing away, lifting a hand in farewell.

He paused before striding resolutely toward the now-empty truck. Something about that seemed reluctant to Ann, as if he didn't want to part company with her. Or was she projecting her own feelings onto him?

Shaking her head at her own foolishness, she hurried around the second truck. As she did so, she heard Dean's workers talking.

"Purely ridiculous," one of them was saying, "tottering around out here on those spiky little heels, all that heavy makeup. She's really come along, though."

"I'll say. I thought she might be kinda cute under all that gilding."

"Dean thinks she's downright hot."

Ann caught her breath and quickly adjusted her route before they saw her.

Was it true? Did Dean think she was hot now?

She didn't know if she was more shaken by the idea that he might truly find her attractive or the unmistakable opinion of his men that she looked better today in her utilitarian ranch clothing than in the expensive designer wardrobe that she usually wore. Suddenly she remembered Dean's comment the day she'd bought these clothes.

You're the girl who rocked a pair of cleats and a batting helmet.

Could he really have found her appealing even then?

I like the real you better.

He'd said that when he'd come to pick up his first check. He'd also called her a snob.

And he hadn't been wrong.

She'd known it, to her shame, at the time, though she hadn't wanted to admit it, especially not to herself. Secretly, she'd felt justified in her attitude, even while knowing better. What had made her think that she could raise herself by looking down on those she'd left behind? That was what it had amounted to.

War Bonnet was small and simple, its folk goodhearted and unpretentious. In many ways life here seemed slower and less complicated than that to which she had become accustomed. Strangely, it also felt less lonely, despite the dozens and dozens of employees, coworkers, guests and friends who surrounded her every day in Dallas.

As she stepped up onto the porch, she caught sight of her father's drawn face in the living room window. He smiled and nodded, obviously eager to hear what Dean had said to her. Strangely, Ann found herself eager to discuss it with him.

How could she have forgotten the ease with which she and her father had conversed and worked together? When had she lost that precious connection with him? Ashamed that it had taken a life-threatening illness to reestablish their relationship, she silently prayed for forgiveness for her neglect of her father and her baseless feelings of superiority. As she removed her shabby baseball cap and hung it on the wall peg, she begged God to spare her dad's life. She had ten years of foolishness to make up for.

Even as she turned to her dad and began to report on Dean's progress, she knew that she needed to speak with her fiancé about their future. Things had changed, and Jordan needed to know.

She made the call immediately after dinner, while Meredith settled Wes into his bed. The call went to voice mail, but before she could make her way back downstairs, her phone rang. Seeing Jordan's photo on her screen, she walked out onto the porch and sat cross-legged on the swing to answer.

"Hi. How are you?"

"Busy," came the terse reply. "You?"

"Things have calmed down a bit. Dad's feeling better every day. The oat harvest is in. We start building the feed mixing station tomorrow. Then we can start the sorghum—"

"That's all very interesting," Jordan cut in, sounding anything but interested. "Unfortunately I've got a situation on my hands here, and I need to resolve it. We booked three gold level suites this weekend and only have two available."

"That's an easy fix," Ann said. "Move into my apartment and give your suite to the third guest."

Silence. Then a chuckle. "Of course. That's why we need you back here. You always see every problem with such clear-eyed perspective and come up with the easiest, most common-sense solutions."

Ann smiled, but then she sighed. "I only wish that were true. Jordan, we have to talk about where we're going to live. I know I said it didn't matter to me, but I don't want to move any farther away from my dad than Dallas."

"You know LHI wants you here in Dallas," he said easily. "So I don't see a problem."

Dropping her feet to the floor, Ann sat up straight. "That's great for me, Jordan, but what about you?"

"Hmm, well, Marshal said something recently about Arizona."

Shocked, Ann yelped, "Arizona!"

Marshal Benton, the CEO of Luxury Hotels, Inc., and Jordan were great friends. Jordan had a gift for befriending people, and he could keep a confidence better than anyone. When she had worked for Jordan, Ann had felt that they were great friends. He was one of the very few people to whom she had poured out her heart, so it shouldn't have been surprising that this was the first she'd heard of Arizona. Except...

"Don't you think that's something your fiancée should be consulted about?"

"It wouldn't be permanent," Jordan said in a soothing tone. "He has in mind a sort of research and development position. I'd be scouting out spots for new hotels, including possible purchases of existing properties, and reporting directly to him. After Arizona, they're looking at Idaho and Seattle."

"So you'd be traveling."

"That's right."

"But Jordan, I thought once we married—"

"Ann," he interrupted, "did you miss the part about me reporting *directly* to Marshal? This is a vice presidency. I don't have to tell you how huge that is. Besides, it's not like we're in a rush to set up housekeeping in a little bungalow with a white picket fence somewhere and fill it with kids. That's not us. Right?"

Donovan's grubby little face flashed before Ann's mind's eye. She thought of the way he threw himself into every hug, of that snaggle-toothed smile beaming up at her and the supreme confidence with which he barreled through each day. If ever a little boy knew he was loved, Donovan did. In that moment she could almost feel the coarseness of his flaming red hair, packed with sand, beneath her fingertips.

You sure are pretty.

Her heart turned over in her chest.

She realized belatedly that Jordan was still talking about his proposed vice presidency, but suddenly she couldn't bear to hear any more.

"I'm sorry," she interrupted, pushing up to a standing position. "I need to check on Dad."

"Ah. All right. Well, I'll move into your rooms

tonight. Give housekeeping a chance to really go over my suite."

"That's fine," she said, just wanting to end the call.

"We'll, um, reconvene when you head back this way."

"Yes. Sounds reasonable."

"Don't make it too long, Ann. Please," he said smoothly. "You're needed and missed here."

She wondered why that felt so sadly impersonal, but she merely said, "Thanks," and hung up. What, she asked herself, had happened to the ambitious career woman who would have rejoiced at this news? More to the point, what had happened to the simple, happy girl who had once lived here? And did some part of her still exist?

Chapter Seven

What was it, Dean wondered, about mornings that made sound carry so clearly? Or had he unknowingly been listening for the rasp and thud of the door on the ranch house across the road? Either way, he didn't have to be told who headed this way, along the meandering path beneath the trees to the shallow ditch beside the road and then across it to the field just south of the barn.

Mentally congratulating himself for keeping his focus on the job at hand, he scraped up a metal washer with gloved fingers and awkwardly maneuvered it onto the second of two bolts sticking up out of the yard-square concrete pad and held out his hand for the metal "foot" that Donovan was even then passing to him. Dean worked the holes in the L-shaped foot over the bolts protruding from the concrete pad and picked up a pair of metal nuts to spin onto the threads of the bolts. Using a wrench, Dean tightened the nuts.

With two such feet now in place, he need only to secure two more. Then he could attach legs to the feet, which together would support the mixing pan with its interior paddle wheel, dump chute and openings for input channels from each of the feed storage bins. By simply manipulating levers on the channels, Rex, Wes or the ranch hands could accurately measure the amount of oats and sorghum that they wished to mix. Dumping the feed from the mixing pan into a truck or trailer bed would be a simple matter of pulling a lever.

Well aware that Ann had arrived on the scene, Dean rose and nodded in greeting, prepared to move to the next corner of the concrete mixing station foundation. Instead, both his jaw and the wrench dropped.

Gone was the snooty hotelier who wouldn't be seen without her perfect makeup and designer clothing. In her place stood a softer, calmer woman, her vibrant hair lying in a braid across her shoulder. Wearing nothing more than mascara and lightly tinted lip gloss, her pale, pearly skin showed the faint stippling of freckles. She might have been seventeen again in her jeans and plaid shirt tied at the waist over a bright blue tank top. For a moment Dean couldn't think, couldn't move, couldn't breathe.

Then he reached up and resettled his cap, hearing himself say, "There's the girl I've missed all this time."

She laughed, almost as if relieved, and closed the distance between them in swift, long strides. For once, Donovan did not throw himself at her, his head swiveling back and forth between them, curiosity sparking in his brilliant eyes. Hearing her laughter, Dean could not restrain himself. He shook off his gloves and reached out his hands to her, which she took without the slightest hesitation. Only his son's presence kept Dean from pulling her into his arms. Still, as her shoulder bumped into his and she smiled up at him, he bent his head toward hers. Only when his thumb brushed over her engagement ring was he able to check himself. Even then he couldn't let the moment pass without comment.

"Welcome home, Jolly," he said softly, smoothing her cheek with one hand as his thumb swept over her engagement ring with the other. "It's good to finally see you."

Her sky-blue eyes plumbed his for a moment. Then Donovan stepped forward, her faded old cap in hand.

"Miss Ann, you dropped something."

"So I did," Ann said, smiling. "Thank you,

Donovan." She took the cap, slapped it onto her head and reached out to drag the boy in for a hug.

Dean found himself swallowing down a sudden lump in his throat and immediately got back to work. He expected her to ask an obligatory question or two and take her leave, but to his surprise, she didn't just stick around, she pitched in. When next he reached for a washer, Ann beat him to it, saving him the trouble of having to scrape it up with the seam of his glove.

After he'd gotten all four metal feet secured, he went to the dually to lift the metal legs from the truck bed. Four feet long and made of heavy, V-shaped channeling, the legs connected to the feet via flattened flanges at the bottoms. They were too heavy for Donovan, even one at a time, so Dean gave him the job of dispensing the bolts, washers and nuts, filling his pockets with each.

"Where's your extra help today?" Ann asked, helping him lay out the legs at each corner of the foundation.

"Tending their own business. They're all small ranchers and farmers around here just picking up an extra buck when they can. I don't need them for this. Doesn't make sense to pay someone to basically hand me what won't fit in my tool belt."

He picked up the first leg, crouched, rested the upper portion against his shoulder and lined up the holes in the flanges on the leg and foot before holding out his gloved hand for the first bolt. Donovan dropped it into his palm, and Dean began working it through the two holes, leaning this way and that to keep the leg lined up. Seeing his problem, Ann walked around behind him and grasped the top of the leg, holding it steady in position.

"Looks to me like you could use an extra pair of hands, though."

Dean shoved the bolt home. "You looking for a job?"

"So what if I am? You hiring?"

He placed the washer and spun on a nut before tilting his head back and smiling up at her. "Depends. How cheap do you work?"

Her eyes narrowed, lips skewing to one side. "Hmm. Job like this... Can't settle for anything less than smiles and hugs."

Dean chuckled and winked at Donovan. "We've got those to spare. Don't we, son?"

Donovan put his head back and beamed a snaggle-toothed smile at Ann, who laughed. It was as if the years literally fell away, but this time, Dean mused, he was part of her crowd, not just hanging around the periphery.

Working together, they quickly got the legs bolted into place. Dean brought out the ladder and set the square metal brace that spaced the top of the legs and held the mixing pan. This part had to be riveted then welded into place, which required significant strength. The first time that the ladder rocked, Ann caught hold of it and made sure that it stood solidly in place while he fixed the rivets.

His welding kit was small, perhaps too small. He hadn't wanted to rent the larger welder, however, when he had a perfectly usable small welder. Unfortunately the small welder couldn't sit on the ground, but was too large for the top of the ladder. Dean started thinking aloud about building a platform.

"Can the brace hold the mixing pan as it is?" Ann asked.

"Sure, but it won't hold several hundred pounds of fodder like this."

"But it will hold that welder, won't it?"

He realized suddenly what she was saying and grinned. "You use that head for more than just a place to park that pretty face, don't you?"

She blushed, actually blushed, and he realized that he was flirting.

"I've never been told that I was stupid," she countered drily.

"No, ma'am, you are not," he agreed, going for the mixing pan.

The pan itself was fairly lightweight, especially without the mixer, chutes and door attached. It was, however, cumbersome. Ann hurried over and helped him carry it by the chute openings to the station. She then shoved as he hauled the pan up the ladder. Getting it wrestled into place proved a feat. He could've done it, but it went much more quickly because Ann climbed the ladder to help him. They performed a strange dance there four feet above the ground, arms over, under and around, bodies shifting and sliding.

When they were done, and the pan was at last appropriately seated, Ann had somehow worked her way to the inside and moved up a rung, turning her back to the ladder, so that they stood pressed together on that narrow structure, staring into each other's eyes. He had pocketed his sunglasses, and she had knocked off her cap again. With one movement he could have gathered her fully against him and kept her there. The impulse was so strong that he slid his hands across her shoulder blades. Her lips parted, and she seemed to be drawing in breath in preparation for his kiss.

Then Donovan called, "You dropped your hat again," and Dean realized that he'd almost kissed Ann Billings on a ladder in the middle of a field in broad daylight with his son running around below them. The engaged-to-be-married Ann Billings.

Dean jumped backward off the ladder, landing with a huff in the red dirt. As he gathered his welding gear, he was exquisitely aware of Ann carefully turning on the ladder and descending step by step. He wasted no time climbing that ladder again, this time to deposit his welding gear in the newly placed pan. Ann passed him the helmet and long gloves necessary for the job.

"You two back away," he ordered, "and do not look directly at the welding arc. Hear me, Donovan? You can damage your eyes looking at that bright light."

"Yessir."

"Let's get a drink," Ann said to the boy, sliding an arm over his shoulders. She walked him to the back of the truck and let down the tailgate to get at the water cooler while Dean struck a spark and ignited the torch.

He took his time with the welding, moving his ladder as necessary. Ann and Donovan sat on the tailgate of his truck with Digger, swinging their legs and talking. He couldn't hear what they were saying, but he saw the way Donovan leaned against her from time to time and heard their occasional laughter. The thought came to him that she would make a wonderful wife and mother.

But not for him and Donovan.

That rock on her finger told him well enough

that he had nothing to offer her. He could never afford a ring like that, never give her the kind of life she was accustomed to, the kind of life she deserved. He was still that silly freshman boy dreaming about a girl who remained worlds above him.

After he finished the welding, Ann and Donovan returned to help him finish installing the mixing pan. They formed an efficient team. Donovan had worked with his father long enough to know each tool by name and which one was used for which job. He passed the correct tool to Ann, who handed it up the ladder to Dean, saving Dean many steps and much time. As a result, the job was finished sooner than expected. Donovan was jubilant.

"We get to go fishin' after, right, Dad?"

"That was the deal," Dean confirmed, stowing the last of his gear in the toolbox in his truck bed. "If we finished early enough, we'd go fishing."

"Ann helped so she can go, too, can't she?" Donovan suggested happily.

Hope and excitement leaped inside Dean, but he kept his face impassive. "Sure. If she wants to."

Ann grinned and ruffled Donovan's bright hair, saying, "I'd like that, but I need to be here for my dad so my sister can take care of some errands."

Dean told himself that it was just as well and his disappointment was entirely out of proportion to the situation, which highlighted his personal foolishness where Ann was concerned. He wasn't fourteen anymore, after all. As a boy, he'd learned that wishing didn't make a thing so. It was past time that he gave up this juvenile fantasy of him and Ann Billings.

"If you'll come to the house, I'll write your check," she was saying. "The amounts were all spelled out in your agreement with Rex."

Nodding, he lifted a hand to indicate that she should lead the way. Donovan and the dog fell into step beside him. Ann walked backward much of the time, chatting with Donovan about what sort of fish he hoped to catch and whether he baited his own hooks.

"'Course I do!" Donovan declared, glancing up at Dean.

"He tries," Dean clarified. "He's certainly not squeamish about it. The only question is whether or not there's enough of the worm left to stay on the hook."

Ann wrinkled her nose. "Gotcha."

"They squish real easy," Donovan muttered, and Dean bit his lip to keep from laughing while Ann delicately shuddered.

They reached the porch, and Dean pointed to the cushioned porch swing, speaking to his son. "Why don't you and Digger enjoy the swing while I go inside with Miss Ann?"

"Aw, Da-a-d," Donovan whined.

Ann ruffled his hair again. "I'm sorry," she apologized, "but my father is very ill, and he can't be around too many people right now. Or dogs."

Donovan's eyes widened solemnly. "What's wrong with him?"

"It's called cancer."

Frowning up at her, Donovan asked, "You're not going to get it, are you?"

"No, no." Ann smiled. "No one can get cancer from someone else, but cancer patients can get all sorts of illnesses from other people while they're getting treatment. He'll be better before long, then you can visit him. In fact, I'm sure he'd like that."

Mollified, Donovan crawled up onto the swing. Digger hopped up next to him, and Donovan began to swing them both as Ann and Dean went into the house.

"I won't be long," Dean promised.

They headed straight into the office, Ann hanging her cap on a peg in the entry hall on the way. Dean swept off his own cap and stuffed the soft part into his hip pocket. She went to the desk, checked something on the computer and got out the checkbook.

"You know," she said, scribbling away, "I wouldn't mind seeing your business plan."

Shocked, Dean chuckled. "Business plan? What business plan?"

"Surely you have one," Ann commented, signing the check. "Everyone does these days." She began carefully tearing the check out of the book. "I don't mean to be nosy. It's just that I find what you do fascinating, and I'd like to see how it all works. I mean your agreement with Rex is very finely drawn."

Dean hung his thumbs in his belt loops. "Jolly, Rex is a lawyer. He drew the agreement. Seemed fair to me, so I signed it. The closest thing I have to a business plan is a budget."

She leaned back in the old desk chair, staring up at Dean. "Seriously?"

He shrugged. "Unless you consider prayer a business plan."

"Dean!" she exclaimed, rocking up onto her feet. "You're smarter than that."

"Apparently, I'm not," he admitted testily, yanking his thumbs free. "There wasn't time for things like business plans and market studies when I started. I didn't expect to be a father at twenty, but that didn't change the fact that when Donovan was born, I had to make money

as quickly as possible. I had land but no equip
ment because Grandpa had bought all the ma
chinery on time-share and it all went back to the
manufacturer when he got sick. I had no credi
of my own, so I sold most of the land, bough
some equipment and went to work farming fo
others. It's just that simple."

"I understand," she told him, handing ove
his check. As he folded the check and slipped i
into his shirt pocket, she said, "But it's not too
late, you know. A good business plan could grow
your business significantly."

He shook his head. "Look, I'm not like you.
didn't finish college, so I work with my hands
Grandma and I stretch every dollar as far as
it will possibly go. And too often it doesn't go
far enough. But we manage, and at least I don'
have any debt."

"I think you could do better than manage,"
Ann suggested gently. "Who carries your line
of credit?"

Exasperated, he snorted. "Haven't you been
listening? I don't have a line of credit, and I don'
care to. I may not be making lots of money, bu
at least I'm not in debt."

"A line of credit isn't about debt," she pointed
out patiently. "It's about leveling out your monthly
income and normalizing your budget so you don'
get caught short. You have more than enough o

a track record now to apply for a line of credit, so if you want, I could take a look at your books, help you draw up a business plan and secure that line of credit so you don't have to worry about months with no income."

Thunderstruck by both the implications and the offer, Dean's first instinct was to refuse. He'd been operating on his own for five years now, and he was who he was, a simple, hardworking man. If that wasn't good enough for her, well, when had it ever been?

On the other hand, how stupid would he be to turn down expert help just because his pride had been pricked? And if there was a way to even out his monthly income so he didn't find himself completely broke at the worst time of the year, he owed it to his son to at least investigate the possibilities. Besides, as foolish as it seemed, when he came right down to it, he wasn't sure he could refuse the opportunity to spend more time with her.

He swallowed his refusal and his pride with it. Nodding, he said, "I'll, uh, be on another job for a few days. Then I've got to get that sorghum cut for the Straight Arrow. Will you be available after that?"

She nodded decisively. "I will."

He felt a rush of relief. "Great. Thank you."

She put out her hand and he took it, shaking

to seal the pact. She smiled suddenly, and it was all he could do not to pull her into his arms for a hug. Instead, he dropped her hand like a hot potato and turned toward the door.

"Okay if I look in on Wes before I leave? I won't get too close."

"Sure. Go on back," she said. "He might be asleep, though."

"I'll be quiet," Dean promised, "just in case."

He strode away, passing Meredith as she came down the stairs, the strap of her handbag on her shoulder.

"All done for the day?" she asked.

"Yep. Just going to say hi to your dad before we head out."

Mindful of Donovan waiting on the porch, Dean didn't pause. He journeyed on down the hall, tiptoeing up to the open doorway of Wes's room. He found the older man in his bed watching television. The grayness of Wes's skin troubled Dean, but he put on a cheery smile and hailed Wes from the doorway.

"How you doing, Mr. Billings?"

The other man cleared his throat. "It's Wes. And I'm doing fine."

He didn't look fine, but Dean said only, "Good to hear it. The mixing station is all done. I think you're going to be real happy with it."

"I'm sure we will be. We're always happy with your work."

"I appreciate you saying so. I'll get started on that sorghum by midweek."

Wes gave him a tired smile. "We'll look forward to seeing you then."

"If you need me before that, you just call. Ann knows how to reach me."

Wes nodded wearily. "Good of you."

"I'll let you rest," Dean said, turning away.

"See you soon," Wes rasped.

When Dean looked back, the older man's eyes were closed as if he'd fallen asleep. Dean stood there a moment longer, until he was sure that Wes's chest rose and fell in regular breaths, before he slipped back down the hall to report to Ann.

"He's sleeping now."

"Did you get to speak to him?" Ann asked.

"A bit. You'll call me if I'm needed, won't you?"

She nodded, smiling slightly. "I wish Rex would get back. If Dad falls or collapses…"

"You just call me," Dean stated flatly. "Anytime. Wherever I am, whatever I'm doing, I'll come. You have my word on it."

"Thank you."

"Save it for when—if—I actually do something."

"I feel better just knowing I can call on you if I need to," she told him.

"Anytime."

He meant it. Anytime Ann called, he'd come, no matter why or when. Even if he was fishing.

That said something sad and rather pathetic about him, but so be it. He could fight his attraction to Ann and his disappointment that she would never feel the same way about him that he felt about her. He could tell himself that he was being foolish and unrealistic. He could pray for wisdom and strength. But he couldn't change who and what he was; in truth, he wouldn't want to try.

One thing being Donovan's father had taught Dean was to be himself. Only by being his authentic self could he help his son grow into his true self. Knowing one's true self was a necessity. Sharing one's true self with another was a gift, an act of love and trust.

It saddened Dean to think that Ann would never know the deepest, truest parts of him, but she was meant for another.

He stepped out onto the porch and pulled the door of the ranch house closed behind him. "Let's go catch some fish."

His son's bright smile lightened his heart.

It was enough. It had to be enough.

Chapter Eight

Ann had known difficult days but nothing like those immediately following the construction of the mixing station. That very evening after Dean left, Wes ate something that didn't agree with him, and within the hour an unrelenting nausea set in. Several times Ann picked up the phone to call Dean, but in truth he could do nothing that Meredith wasn't already doing. Just because having Dean there would make *her* feel better was no reason for Ann to call him over to the house, especially as she had no right to the comfort and support he offered.

In fact, having Dean around was dangerous. She'd come to realize that he was dangerous to her heart, as well as her peace of mind. That didn't keep her from hoping that he'd stop by to check on Wes.

In a very real way, she missed Dean. She'd

sort of gotten used to seeing him on a daily basis. Yet, her father was so ill that Ann didn't feel comfortable leaving Meredith alone with him and going to church on Sunday.

By Sunday evening both sisters were worn to frazzles, and Wes seemed no better. Meredith had already consulted Dr. Alice Shorter by telephone, and she called the doctor again, as instructed, very early on Monday morning. Dr. Shorter drove out to the ranch straightaway, bringing intravenous medications with her.

On the plump side and fiftyish, with long, straight, thick blond hair, Dr. Shorter had a dry, ready wit, remarking to Wes, "If you wanted to see me, Billings, you didn't have to go to such extremes. You could've just invited me to dinner."

Wes chuckled then clutched his loudly rumbling belly with one hand. "Don't even…mention…food."

"Sorry. Let's get you comfortable."

While Meredith set up the IV, Dr. Shorter conducted a routine examination before announcing, "Well, you're dehydrated. No surprise there. We'll get some fluids and medication in you and calm this down." She nodded at Meredith, adding, "At least your nurse knows her stuff."

"She's good," Wes managed with a smile.

Meredith didn't even look up from securing the IV in her father's arm.

Watching from the foot of the bed, Ann said, "We're lucky to have her."

"Blessed," Wes corrected. "I'm blessed…with both…my daughters."

Ann smiled at that, glad she could at least be here to help run the ranch while Rex was gone. She couldn't care for their dad the way Meri did, but at least she could contribute in some ways. And to think that in the beginning she had secretly resented having to put her life on hold to come here and do this. The selfishness of that shamed her, and she was deeply, deeply grateful for this time with her father and sister.

"What set you off?" the doctor asked.

Wes made his face, flattening his lips in a stubborn expression that she knew all too well, so Ann answered for him.

"Catfish. He had an intense craving for it. We thought it would be mild enough for him, so we brought it in from the diner."

"The fish, maybe," the doctor said. "The grease it's fried in, probably not."

"I should have thought of that," Meredith said guiltily. "Callie would have."

"Callie had training, if I'm not mistaken," Dr. Shorter pointed out. She poked Wes in the chest with a gloved forefinger then, adding, "And so did you."

He rolled his eyes. "Sounded…*so* good."

The doctor turned to her kit and found a syringe. "Doesn't feel so good now, does it?"

"Nope."

His poor stomach rumbled so loudly that the doctor handed him the basin sitting on the bedside table. "Need to puke?"

Wes gritted his teeth, swallowed and closed his eyes. "No."

Alice Shorter shook her head and injected medication into his IV tube, muttering, "Men and their pride."

"Not pride," Wes ground out. "Self-respect."

She patted his shoulder. "I forgot. Christians are forbidden pride. Have it your way."

"You know… I will," Wes said, one corner of his mouth hitching up in a smile.

Ann could tell that he was already beginning to relax. To her surprise, the doctor reached down and squeezed his hand. Even more surprising, he grasped her hand and held it for several long seconds. The three women—Ann, her sister and Dr. Alice Shorter—stood quietly around his bed until he began to breathe easily and slipped into peaceful sleep. Meredith's hands trembled as she smoothed her light golden brown hair back from her face and twisted it into a long rope.

"It's different when it's family, isn't it?" Dr. Shorter said softly, and Ann recognized the sound of experience in her voice. Meredith nodded.

Abruptly, the doctor began packing up her bag. A few seconds later she stripped off her gloves and dropped them in the trash can. Then she was heading for the door.

"He'll sleep for a while. Call me if you need me."

"Thank you, Dr. Shorter," Meredith murmured, following the older woman from the room, Ann on her heels.

They picked up the pace in the hallway, but the doctor was out the door before they could catch up to her. Wandering back into the kitchen, where her sister went to the refrigerator for the tea pitcher, Ann brought her hands to her hips and thought over all that had just happened.

"Do you know," she said after a moment, "I think Dr. Shorter might have a crush on Dad."

Meredith looked around, taking an ice tray from the freezer, and she raised her eyebrows. "Don't be silly. I've heard that she's an atheist, and you know Dad's a very outspoken Christian."

"He's also a very attractive man, even ill."

Meredith shook her head, cracking the ice tray over the sink. "Doesn't mean anything. He would never be interested in her."

"No? Meri, Mom's been gone since 2012. What would be wrong with Dad finding someone else?"

"Nothing." Meredith dropped ice cubes into glasses. "I hope he does. Once he's well again."

And what if he's never well? Ann wondered. Doesn't he deserve every moment of happiness he can find, well or not?

The house phone rang, and Meredith reached out to answer it.

After greeting whoever was on the other end and a moment of chatter, she said, "Ann's right here. Want her to take this in the office?" She held the telephone receiver away from her ear and said to Ann, "It's Rex. I'll bring your tea to you."

"Thanks, sis."

Ann hurried to the office and picked up the cordless receiver there. She listened while Meredith filled in Rex on their dad's most recent health issues. Then Meri hung up on her end, and Ann and Rex got down to business. Rex had been going over the books online and had some questions. Ann had paid a couple of bills he hadn't expected to come in for several weeks yet, and he wanted to see the statements. Meredith brought her iced tea while Ann was scanning up and emailing the billing statements. As soon as her sister left the room, Ann took the opportunity to ask Rex about Dean, shading her question in tones of concern.

"Just how much do you know about Dean Paul Pryor? I have a few concerns."

"Problems with his work?" Rex queried, sounding surprised.

"His work is fine, but he doesn't really seem very fiscally sound. I can't help wondering just how much you really know about him."

"I know everything I need to know," Rex insisted. "Dean's as honest as the day is long and the hardest working young man you'll find anywhere."

"I know he works hard," Ann ventured carefully. "He just seems…well, he's awfully young to be a single father."

"That's true, but he didn't have to take responsibility for the boy at all," Rex pointed out. "The mother was a college student, same as Dean. When Dean proved to be the biological father, he took custody of the child, and that was that.

"He might have been a little wild at one point," Rex conceded, "but everyone agrees he's been an excellent father, especially since he became a Christian not long after his boy was born."

"I certainly can't argue that point," Ann said,

trying not to let her smile sneak through into her tone.

"Dean may not be the best businessman, but he's young, and he'll learn," Rex insisted.

"I'm sure you're right," Ann agreed. In fact, she meant to make certain of it by helping Dean learn what he needed to know to solidify and grow his business, starting with a business plan. Business, after all, was what she did best, and a hardworking, loving, responsible father deserved all the expertise and help he could get.

Now she just had to figure out how to protect her silly heart while she helped this handsome single dad make the most of what he did best.

When Dean arrived at the sorghum field at dawn on Wednesday morning, Ann already stood beside her dad's old truck, dressed in running shorts and a tank top, her hair in a ponytail. Waving, she jogged around to the passenger side of the truck and hauled out a square pan covered in a dish towel. Parking the thing on the front fender of the truck, she smiled cheerfully and pointed to it. Dean brought the dually and the combine that it was hauling to a slow, shuddering halt in the center of the narrow, rutted, red dirt road.

She looked better than she had as an eighteen-year-old, all long, slender muscles and womanly curves.

A sleepy Donovan craned his neck to see what had caught his father's attention. His gaze went to the pan on the fender of the Straight Arrow pickup truck, and he happily exclaimed, "She brought food!"

Digger, in the front passenger seat, perked up at that. Dean had to laugh, not just because of his son's and his dog's interest in the food but because he hadn't given that cloth-covered pan a second thought.

"Looks like it."

Leaving the rig where it sat, he killed the engine and got out. By the time he unbuckled Donovan and crossed the ditch to Ann's truck, she had folded back the cloth and the sheet of waxed paper beneath it and helped herself to the biggest sticky bun he'd ever seen.

"Meredith put these up last night," she said around a big bite. She chewed and swallowed before adding, "Since I wasn't about to miss these bad boys, I figured I'd better bring enough for everyone."

Dean figured that he was grinning as broadly as Donovan, who practically soared with glee.

"Can I, Dad?"

"Sure. It'd be rude not to eat these after Miss

Meredith baked them and Miss Ann brought them all the way out here."

"There's no clean way to do it," Ann warned, "so I brought packets of wipes. Dig in."

Dean used his hands to peel off a bun for Donovan then took one for himself. Tasting of butter, brown sugar, cinnamon and pecans, the things practically melted in the mouth—and all over the face and hands. Ann had brought coffee and milk, too. Dean was not a big coffee drinker, but it had never tasted so good as it did that morning.

They ate leaning against the truck, watching the sun play peekaboo over the horizon.

"I meant what I said about the business plan," Ann told him between bites. "If you'd let me look over your books, I think I could help you formulate a good plan and set up a line of credit."

"I told you I'd do it," he reminded her lightly.

"I know. I just thought we could get started sooner rather than later. Like tonight maybe?"

He wondered if she was rushing to get out of town, but then he thought of her dad and discarded the notion. She wouldn't leave until Wes was better and Rex returned, which could be sooner than anyone realized.

"I'll bring the books over tonight," he decided.

She smiled and bit into her sticky bun. He ate three big buns and drank two tall cups of coffee before Donovan, Digger and Ann could finish off their own. To say that Donovan needed a wipe after he was done was akin to calling the Red River a stream.

Ann seemed a little horrified by what she had wrought with her sticky buns. She broke out the wipes and went to work. By the time she was satisfied that the entire Straight Arrow Ranch wouldn't stick to Donovan, her wipes had been all used up. Dean poured the last of the coffee on a ragged bandanna and cleaned himself well enough to proceed with his day. He was going to be dusty and sweaty in an hour's time, anyway. Ann, however, was another story, and her attempts to take care of herself with the used wipes only made matters worse.

She was a good sport about it, and cute as a button in the bargain. Dean could've stood there and watched her wipe and rewipe all day, but they both had work to do. He allowed himself just so much fun before he took her by the arm and walked her to his truck.

"Come with me. I keep a container of baby wipes under the backseat."

"Okay, so I grossly underestimated the number of wipes needed," she admitted, skipping along beside him to the truck.

"Baby wipes are one of mankind's greatest inventions," Dean told her, opening the back door of the dually and reaching inside. He felt around under the seat until he found the cylindrical container and hauled it out. "One of the first things you learn when you have a kid is that you can never have too many baby wipes."

"Got it."

Popping the top, he pulled out two and handed them to her so she could clean her hands. When she had that job whipped, he gave her another wipe for her face, though he really hated to see the sticky, brownish circle around her lips go. He wished he'd taken a picture with his phone. She seemed so far removed from the polished, big-city hotelier who had greeted him that first day, more like his Jolly—if such a person actually existed. She was certainly making a hash of cleaning her face.

"Hold on. Hold on," he said, chuckling. "First of all, fold that thing so the clean side is up."

She looked down at the wipe and folded it. "Okay."

"Now, start here." He touched his own face.

She wiped the wrong cheek.

"No, no. The other cheek."

She moved her hand. "Like this?"

"Almost. To your right. Got it. Now move in. And turn your wipe over."

Exactly as instructed, she turned the wipe over. Then her gaze came back to his, and he pointed to a spot on his own cheek. She lifted her hand to her face once more. He realized only as she slowly swept the wipe over her lips that they were still looking into each other's eyes, and abruptly his breath seized.

Suddenly, as the sun shot golden rays across the fields, igniting tiny fires in the red-orange dirt of the road, they somehow stood apart from the rest of the world, wrapped in an intimate, electric awareness. As if in a trance, Dean lifted his hand and brushed the backs of his fingers against her cheek. Then he turned his hand and lightly cupped the curve of her jaw. She tilted her head ever so slightly, leaning into his palm, her eyelids growing slumberous, lips parting. Emboldened, he slid his hand to the back of her neck and felt her lean toward him.

Then Donovan slammed into his side.

"Dad, Dad! Can I go under the wire with Digger? He's got some armerdiller or ground squirrel over yonder."

The dog's barking finally penetrated Dean's consciousness. "Uh…" Blinking, he stared down at his son and found a reasonable answer. "No. Might be a skunk he's found. Better hang with me until we get the combine into the field."

Donovan dug a toe into the dirt. "Aw."

Ann was already halfway across the road when Dean looked up again. "Rex tied a red flag on the section of fence that can come down," she called. "He's had pipe laid over the ditch so you can drive right over." Of course, Dean could see the movable cattle guards temporarily bridging the ditch.

"Great!" Dean shouted after her, fully aware that she was running away from what had almost happened between them. He didn't blame her. She was engaged to be married, after all. To an older, established, successful man. But Dean couldn't escape the certainty that, given just a moment longer, she would have allowed the kiss that hadn't happened.

In light of that, Dean had to wonder if working on a business plan with her was such a good idea, but even as he wondered, he knew he was going to do it. Somehow, with her, he couldn't seem to help himself. So, that evening after supper, he left Donovan with his grandmother and drove back to the Straight Arrow with his account books.

Meredith answered the door. "Come on in. Annie's on the phone, but Dad would love to see you."

"I'll be happy to visit with him for a few minutes. I promise I won't tire him."

"He's feeling better," Meredith told him. "It'll be fine."

"Thanks for the sticky buns this morning, by the way. They were great, really good."

Meredith shot him a smile over her shoulder as he hung his hat on the wall peg and followed her into the living room. "Callie put them in the freezer before she left. All I had to do was thaw them overnight and shove them in the oven this morning."

"Well, you did a good job of it," Dean insisted politely.

"What you really mean is that sister-in-law of mine can sure cook."

"That, too," Dean admitted with a chuckle.

"Meredith has her own talents," Wes said from his recliner. "She's a top-notch nurse, my Meri."

"Oh, Dad." Meredith patted the top of his bald head affectionately on her way to the kitchen, saying, "Call if you need anything."

Dean couldn't say that Wes looked much improved, but his color wasn't so gray, and something about his smile seemed brighter, healthier. Easing into the room, Dean nodded at his host, who waved him toward the comfortably worn leather sofa. Wes immediately clicked off the television with a remote controller.

Dean sat and stacked his ledgers atop his knees. Wes glanced at them but remarked only, "Ann says the sorghum looks good."

"It does. Rex's timing has been perfect with the harvest."

"Boy's a natural," Wes proclaimed proudly.

"Always suspected it, but it took him a while to figure it out. Well, everyone has to take their own path."

"I hear he's a really good lawyer, too."

"Oh, yeah, he is," Wes stated without hesitation.

Dean had to grin. He knew just how Wes felt about his son, and he was glad that the feeling didn't necessarily fade with time.

"Ann's done a good job for us, too," Wes added, and Dean quickly agreed.

"She has."

"Between you and me, I'm seeing some changes I like in her lately. Not sure that big-city fiancé of hers would approve, but she seems more her true self to me now than she has in a long time."

Dean said nothing, but privately he thought Ann's fiancé a hopeless fool if he didn't completely and wholeheartedly approve of Ann and all she was.

Maybe she wasn't perfect, but no simple human being could be. She was, however, and had been for as long as Dean had known her, all things lovely and fine.

What man in his right mind would not approve of—and appreciate—that?

Conversation had moved to that morning's breakfast of sticky buns, with Wes joking that he'd needed a sponge bath after finishing his, by the time Ann swept into the room. She smiled distractedly at her father and twisted the heavy diamond on her finger in a way Dean had never seen before this. He knew at once that something troubled her.

"You okay?"

She flashed a smile and waved a hand in a gesture that didn't quite appear as careless as it might have. "It's…" She shook her head. "A work thing."

He didn't like to even think about the job waiting for her back in Texas, but he could see that something weighed heavily on her mind just now.

Lifting the slender books in his hands, he suggested, "Maybe I should just leave these with you for now. You can look them over at your convenience and get back to me later."

To his disappointment, she pressed trembling fingertips to her temple and nodded. "Maybe that would be best."

His spirits plummeting, he got to his feet. "I'll let y'all enjoy your evening. It was good to see you, Mr. Wes. Take care now."

Uncertain what to do with the books, he placed them on the coffee table and moved toward the door, sliding sideways past Ann. He'd nearly reached the foyer when she suddenly announced, "I'll walk you out."

Surprised, he stopped then almost wrapped an arm around her waist as she came up next to him; Wes called out a farewell just in time to remind Dean that would not be a good idea. Stuffing his hands into the pockets of his jeans, he tucked his elbows in tight as he stepped into the entry hall with Ann right at his side.

They skirted the stairs in silence. When they reached the foyer, he took his hat from the peg but kept it in one hand, opening the front door with the other, holding it wide until Ann pushed through the screen. She crossed the porch and stepped down onto the well-beaten pathway, but then she paused and waited for him to pull the door closed, sidestep the screen and catch up to her.

Half a dozen innocuous topics of conversation slipped through his mind, but something sat so heavily on hers that he couldn't bring himself to start a conversation. Finally, just as they approached the edge of the trees, she spoke.

"Can I ask you something and get an honest answer?"

Even though little, if any, traffic could be expected along this private road at this time of evening, Dean had pulled his truck to the side of the road nearest the house, parking practically in the shallow bar ditch. He stepped across that narrow ditch, reached in through the open window and laid his hat on the seat of the truck. Turning, he put his back to the passenger's door and leaned against it, folding his arms.

"Sure."

She shook her head with obvious agitation, her eyes gleaming in the dusky light. Darkness often didn't fall until nine o'clock at this time of year, and they had no moon this early in August, only the light of the stars and the ambient illumination from the vapor lights near the barn and the rear of the house. He wondered if the sheen of her eyes could be from tears.

"An *honest* answer," she repeated sternly. "Don't spare my feelings."

He stilled, everything in him focused on this woman before him, this woman he had wanted for so long. His heart pounded as he imagined the questions he *hoped* she would ask.

"I've always been honest with you, Jolly. I always will be. You have my word on that."

He'd never meant any words more than those.

Chapter Nine

Watching her face, Dean knew for certain that Ann was on the verge of tears, but he made himself stay as he was, and finally she came out with it.

"Do you think I'm feminine?"

That couldn't have been what he'd heard. He'd been hoping for something along the lines of, *Do you like me?* or *Do you think of me when we're not together?* or maybe even *Do you think there's a chance for you and me?* But…no, he couldn't have heard her right.

"I beg your pardon?"

Her hands balling into fists, she practically shouted it at him. "Do you think I'm feminine?"

The question was so stupid that for a moment he still couldn't wrap his mind around it. As a result, his tone may have been a bit sharper than he'd intended. "Of course. How could you be anything else?"

She shifted, mirroring his stance with her arms folded. "But what, specifically, is womanly about me?"

"What is—" He nearly swallowed his tongue. When she looked in the mirror, did she not see what he saw when he looked at her? Dropping his arms, Dean slapped his hands against his thighs. "What isn't? Jolly, you're the most—"

Throwing up her hands, she interrupted hotly, declaring, "I have *no* feminine accomplishments. I can't cook. I don't know the first thing about kids. Half the time I can't even figure out how to dress!"

"What's that got to do with anything?" he wanted to know, shoving away from the truck.

"I have no close female friends," she went on. "I can't sew. I can't…grow flowers or make jewelry or…" She whirled her hands in angry circles. "I can't do anything that most women do!"

Dean just stood there, still not believing what he was hearing.

"I'm not like other women," she declared, and he could tell that she was working herself up to a real meltdown about this. Every time he opened his mouth, she spouted something nonsensical about being too masculine or broad-shouldered or tall.

Then she complained about her hair and her freckles.

"What's wrong with red hair and freckles?" He liked red hair and freckles. That was how he'd wound up with a redheaded, freckle-faced son.

"Your face is beautiful, freckles and all," Dean interrupted bluntly, but she couldn't even hear him at this point, having moved on to the color of her eyes, which were apparently "washed out and faded, like old jeans."

Frustrated, Dean did the only thing he could think to do, the thing he most *wanted* to do.

He took one long step, breaching the chasm between them, reached out with both arms and pulled her flush against him, capturing her lips with his.

For an instant, everything froze. But then he tightened his arms and poured everything he had into that kiss, everything he'd felt for so long, everything he wanted with this woman. In seconds she melted, and her arms slid up around his neck.

Kissing Jolly was everything he'd ever dreamed it could be.

Not feminine? He wanted to shake her for being so stupid. Then he felt her smile, and he was lost to the wonder of having her, at last, exactly where he wanted her. Where she surely belonged.

Didn't she?

If that were so, though, why was she suddenly pushing away from him? And laughing.

Frowning, Dean watched her back up a step and raise one hand as if to hold him off. Her laughter faded to a huge grin, but he still didn't like the look of it.

Was she laughing at him?

She clapped her hand to her chest then and said, "That was my fault. I know that men speak with actions more than words, and I didn't exactly give you a chance to really say anything, so you made your point the most efficient way you could. And, well, I just want to thank you."

A chill ran through him, followed by an unexpected surge of white-hot anger that stunned him with its intensity.

"Thank you," he echoed with deadly calm. "That's what you've got to say to me after that kiss? Thank you?"

Her smile faded, and she dropped her hand, moving from gratitude to apology. "I'm sorry. I was having a big old pity party, and I dragged you into it. That wasn't fair."

"You think that was about pity?" he demanded, aware that he was shouting but not quite able to control his tone. She just stared at him, clearly clueless. "You may not have 'feminine accomplishments,' as you call them," he managed, leveraging volume into sarcasm and curling his fingers to indicate quotation marks for emphasis, "and you may be better at some things than most men, but the only *masculine* thing about you is your stubborn, blind, ridiculous inability to see what's right in front of you!"

Her eyebrows jumped into pointed little arches, and she looked down as if expecting to find something sprouting from the ground.

"Uh, I don't—"

"I'm talking about me!" he snapped.

"You?" Her gaze jerked up to meet his.

Parking his hands at his hips, he bluntly admitted, "I've wanted to do that for years."

"You've wanted to kiss me for years?" she squeaked.

"But never more so than recently," he told her, "and I'm tired of you never seeing or acknowledging my—" he almost said *feelings for you,* but he was too much the stubborn, blind, ridiculous male himself to give away that much, especially now, so he settled for "—attraction to you."

She looked stunned as if he'd punched her in the gut, and he suddenly felt completely drained, emotionally and physically.

"Dean," she began, "I didn't… I never…"

The words just died away, and that was it, all he could handle.

"I have to go," he muttered abruptly.

Striding around her, he hopped across the ditch in one long stride and kept right on going until he'd circled the truck and reached the driver's door. She stood as if rooted to the ground while he opened the door, shoved aside his hat and wedged himself inside the slanting truck. After he started the engine, wrenched the steering wheel as far right as it would go and swung the truck in a wide U-turn, he hit the brake. She had followed the motion of the truck but still stood with her arms dangling at her sides, her jaw agape. Shaking his head, Dean pushed the gas pedal and drove away, leaving her there, staring after him.

"Lord, help me," he whispered.

Would he *never* learn? He couldn't just answer her idiotic questions and listen to her rant. He couldn't let it go at the kiss. He'd had to tell her that he'd carried this torch for her for years.

Oh, what had he done? What *had* he done?

What had she done?

Ann watched the red taillights of Dean's truck grow smaller and smaller in the darkening distance, torn between elation and shame.

On one hand, she was thrilled beyond words

that the most masculine man she knew found her attractive. That kiss left no doubt about that. None. She lifted trembling fingers to her lips and found them curved in a smile.

On the other hand, she was an engaged woman, pledged to marry another, and he was the one who should be giving her such thrilling assurances. She should never have dragged Dean into it.

The problem was that when she'd asked Jordan if he thought she was too masculine, he'd replied that what mattered was her *brain*. He'd then gone on to say that she had one of the finest managerial minds he'd ever encountered and how essential she was to the success of the Dallas hotel, which had run a slight deficit before she'd taken over, even with him at the helm. He'd talked about how much she was missed there and asked again how soon she could return. All of his words had been flattering, but the conversation had left her shaken. It had been as if she was talking to her *boss* rather than her fiancé, and doubts had suddenly overwhelmed her. She'd asked herself if Jordan truly loved her or if she was just a wise career choice for him.

Feeling vulnerable and frightened that her perfect future might not be so perfect after all, she'd told herself to steer clear of Dean, but for some reason she hadn't been able to stick to the plan. When Dean had actually gotten up to leave the ranch house, she'd panicked. In some strange way, he had become her anchor in a world that had turned upside down.

Her father's illness, her return to War Bonnet, her growing concerns about her engagement, Rex's continued absence, her confused feelings about Dean and Donovan…it all whirled around her, a tornado of emotion. Even the good things seemed too much all of a sudden. Her success here at Straight Arrow—Rex seemed pleased with the way she'd kept things running—relaxing into a simpler lifestyle, feeling finally as if she'd really come home, reconnecting with her dad and sister, the comfort of church and Christian fellowship somehow piled one atop another until she felt buried by everything that had happened these past few weeks. She'd wanted to grab hold of Dean and never let go again.

But that kiss…

Never in her wildest dreams had she imagined anything like that kiss. Minutes later she still tingled all the way to her toes. Guiltily, she realized that not one of Jordan's few kisses had ever made her feel even remotely like this. She had presumed that she was the problem. After all, hadn't she known for years now that she was not like other women? Or was she?

All through the night she tossed and turned,

torn between the delight of Dean's kiss and al
that it seemed to reveal, and guilt that she hac
enjoyed Dean's kiss so much more than her fiancé's. By morning she had decided that the only
thing to do was to call Jordan and have a frank
talk with him.

She did it early, very early, so she wouldn't in-
terrupt Jordan's working day and in order to give
them the time necessary to say all that needed to
be said. She did it before she even got dressed
Because of the hour, she wasn't surprised that he
didn't answer on the first or second ring. Wher
at last he picked up, she immediately apologized

"I'm sorry to call so early, but we really need
to talk."

"Ann," Jordan groaned. "We spoke just las
night."

"I know, but something's happened."

"Your father?"

"No, no. Me." Drawing her legs up beneath
the bedcovers, she held the cell phone to her
ear. "I, um, kissed someone. Rather," she hurried on, "someone kissed me. But… I—I did..
participate."

She heard dead silence on the other end o
the line.

"Jordan, I'm sorry, but I felt you had a righ
to know."

"Do you want to break our engagement?" Jordan asked carefully.

"Do you?"

"Ann," he said softly, warmly, "these things happen when couples are separated. Given the stress you've been under and the fact that you're a woman working in an almost exclusively male field now…" He sighed. "Well, I can't say I'm happy, but I'm not surprised, either. Just don't let your head be turned by one of the local yokels back there in Oklahoma. Your life is here in Dallas. We can really build something together, Ann. Don't lose sight of us and the future we have. Please. I—I don't think I can do this without you."

Melting, Ann said, "Jordan, that's so sweet."

"It's a onetime thing, right? Just a onetime thing."

She started to tell him that it wouldn't happen again, but she barely got the first two words out before another call rang through. "It won't— Oh, Jordan, I'm sorry. This is my brother. It must be important for him to call so early."

"That's okay, darling," Jordan said. "We can talk again later."

"Thank you. Yes. Just give me a little while to take care of this." She quickly tried to put an end to the call and get to Rex, who sounded harried.

"Oh, good. I caught you before you left the

house," he said as soon as he heard her voice. "I have a delivery of building supplies coming in two weeks earlier than expected. Some sort of scheduling mix-up. The transporter just called to say that his trucker has driven through the night to get to us first thing this morning so he can make another delivery somewhere in north Texas before nightfall."

Rex went on to detail where the supplies needed to be off-loaded and stored, just in case Duffy, whom he'd awakened from a sound sleep, didn't understand or remember his instructions. Then Rex told Ann that she would have to coordinate with Stark Burns, the local veterinarian, who had partnered with Rex on the order so they could take advantage of a bulk discount. Only after Stark deemed the order complete would Rex transfer payment to the supplier.

"I'll call him after we hang up," Ann promised. Because she hadn't seen their father yet this morning, they had nothing to talk about there, so she ended the call.

Only then did she realize that she'd accidentally put Jordan on hold. Remembering her parting words to him, that she just needed a little while to take care of Rex's call, she feared that Jordan was still on the line.

Swiping the correct button, she spoke. "Jordan, I'm so sorry. I didn't mean for you to hold."

The line was open, and she did hear him speak but distantly. "Don't know," he was saying, "and I don't care. Some dusty, drawling redneck, I imagine."

Ann heard another voice, a feminine one, but she didn't recognize it or understand the words until the speaker came closer. "Doesn't seem her type," the woman said, and Ann suddenly knew to whom that voice belonged. Gena Johns, one of the customer service clerks who worked the main reception desk. But what was Gena doing in Jordan's—Ann's—suite at this time of the morning?

"Who *is* her type?" Jordan was asking, his tone dry.

"You, obviously," Gena answered, sounding petulant.

"Guess that's why Marshal gave me this assignment," Jordan said, his voice growing louder then fading as if he bent toward the phone and backed off again.

Assignment? Ann thought, freshly stunned as Jordan asked Gena to hand him his shirt. *What assignment?*

As the ramifications of what she was hearing began to sink in, Ann dropped the phone into her lap. This couldn't mean what it seemed to mean. Could it? Tears filling her eyes, she shook her head. It was a mistake. She'd misunderstood.

Gingerly, she picked up the phone again and held it to her ear.

"…believe she's still buying it," Jordan was saying, "but I may need to move up the wedding date."

"You said you'd jilt her before it got too far," Gena whined.

Ann closed her eyes, horrified.

"That *was* the plan," Jordan said. "If it could be done before the wedding arrangements were too far underway. But things change."

"You're really going to marry her?" Gena demanded.

"If that's what it takes to get her back here and keep her with LHI," Jordan answered bluntly.

Ann slapped a hand over her mouth as a sound of horror escaped her.

"Look," Jordan said calmly, "if her father hadn't gotten sick, she wouldn't be playing cowgirl in Dirtville now and none of this would be necessary. But it's like Marshal says, we can't take the chance that her family will guilt her into staying on to run the family business. I promised him I'd get her back here ASAP, and trust me when I tell you this is the way to do it."

He would know, of course. Ann had told him exactly how to guarantee her cooperation.

"I've got a huge promotion riding on this," Jordan went on. "So if I have to drive down to that waste of space again to sell it and march her up the wedding aisle to get her back here, that's what I'll do. Not that it matters much because I'll be living in another state, anyway."

Ann couldn't bear to hear any more. Crushed, tears coursing down her face, she broke the connection and fell back on the bed.

An assignment. A project. A promotion deal. That's all she was to Jordan, all she'd ever been.

Some small, sane part of her supposed that she ought to be flattered because Marshal Benton and Luxury Hotels, Inc., thought enough of her to go to such lengths to keep her on the job. Such filthy, underhanded, sneaky, hateful lengths. And she'd given them the nefarious plan herself.

It all made terrible sense now. Jordan had shown up in Dallas not long after her dad's cancer had been confirmed. Ostensibly, he had come to relieve her so she could take off time to help out here at the Straight Arrow, but he'd needed to be brought up to speed before she could leave the hotel *that he had managed before she had taken over.* Of course, he'd used that time to sweep her off her feet and get an engagement ring on her finger, ensuring that she'd return to Dallas as quickly as possible— long after she'd confessed her personal history and fears to him. And she'd fallen for the whole charade, hook, line and sinker.

Foolish didn't begin to cover her idiocy.

Ann turned facedown into her pillow and sobbed, her entire world shattering around her.

She had believed that Jordan loved her.

She had thought that he wanted her for herself.

She had trusted in the future that he had promised her. Maybe it wouldn't have been quite traditional. Maybe she wouldn't have been a mother or a homemaker, but she'd have been a wife, a partner, half of a couple.

Or so she'd thought.

In truth, she was nothing more to Jordan Teel than a means to an end, an assignment that he meant to leave behind at the first opportunity.

Only one man, it seemed, had ever seen her as a woman, and now she had to wonder if even that could be real. Maybe all Dean wanted was a mother for his son. At best he might want Jolly, the silly, thoughtless girl Ann used to be. He didn't really know the person she was now. How could he when she wasn't sure that she knew herself anymore?

She couldn't trust anyone or anything right now.

For the first time, her soul felt as dry as kindling.

Oh, Father God, help me! she cried silently,

but her prayers seemed to bounce off the ceiling and fall back to her shoulders, driving her deeper into despair.

Eventually she heard the long blast of a horn and realized that the hauler with the building supplies about which Rex had warned her had arrived. Pulling herself together enough to crawl out of the bed, she pulled on jeans, boots and a nondescript T-shirt then found her phone and dragged herself out of the room without so much as glancing at a mirror.

She was creeping down the upstairs hall and looking up the veterinarian's phone number when that horn blasted again. Meredith stepped out of her room, belting her robe over her pajamas.

"What's going on?"

"Mix-up with a delivery schedule," Ann explained dully, moving toward the stairs. Meredith caught her by the arm, turning her back.

"You okay? You don't look well, Annie."

"Couldn't sleep last night," Ann muttered. "Then Rex called early. Gotta go."

She tapped the number displayed on the screen of her telephone and let it dial Stark Burns's number. Meredith's hand fell away as Ann turned once more for the stairs, lifting the phone to her ear.

Burns sounded wide-awake when he answered

the call. Ann told him what was needed, and he replied that he was on his way. She flipped on porch lights to let the trucker outside know that she would be with him momentarily then trudged across the porch and along the path to the road. To her surprise, what awaited her was a full-blown tractor-trailer rig with a skid loader on the back.

By the time Ann and the driver figured out how best to position the trailer to off-load the materials meant for the Straight Arrow, Duffy had arrived. Burns quickly followed in a one-ton flatbed truck. After Burns agreed that the order was complete, the trucker agreed to load certain bundles onto Burns's truck if Rex verbally signed off on the arrangement and put through payment.

Ann contacted Rex, who took care of his end of things, and the trucker proved he knew his business by quickly off-loading his shipment then backing the rig straight down that red-dirt road well over half a mile before he could turn it around and head it south to Texas. Burns, in his usual taciturn manner, wrote a check for his part of the order and took himself off again.

Ann dragged back into the house to face Meredith's frown. "What was that man doing here?"

"Which one?"

"That so-called animal doctor."

Meredith could not forgive Burns for failing to save her injured cat. Ann sighed and explained about the building supplies, then for the first time in memory, she decided to forgo her Thursday morning run. Instead, she took a long shower then got dressed again and went downstairs to face her family with wet hair and red-rimmed eyes.

Fortunately Meredith had already related her tale of a sleepless night, bungled scheduling and early-morning calls, so their dad commiserated rather than questioned.

No one seemed to notice her missing engagement ring, which sat atop her dresser, boxed, addressed, and waiting to be brought to the War Bonnet post office.

Chapter Ten

Missing. Dean expected Ann to show up in the field every day, but the woman had gone missing.

She had always been the gutsy type, but obviously that kiss had driven her away, maybe all the way back to Texas. He had a perfect excuse, the business plan, to stop by the house, but he couldn't quite work up the courage. If she didn't want to see him, he was not about to force his company on her.

Yet he felt a burning need, which only grew as time passed, to at least clap eyes on her. Part of him needed to know that she was well; part of him needed to know that she didn't hate him or, even worse, scorn him. Mostly he just wanted to see her. Sometimes he wondered how he had gone for so many years without just *seeing* her. They didn't even have to talk; he just needed to look at her and know that she still existed in the world.

The wounded part of him felt some residual anger over her reaction to that kiss, but then he closed his eyes to sleep at night and the memory of it washed over him afresh. He remembered the feel of her in his arms, and he couldn't help smiling.

If only she hadn't thanked him, hadn't suggested it was all about pity.

If only he hadn't carried the image in his head all these years of this vibrant, laughing, confident, beautiful girl who could melt him with a careless smile and knock a ball out of the park with the same ease. No other girl he'd ever met had measured up to her.

And she'd wanted to know if she was feminine!

He still wished he'd shaken her. Right after he'd kissed her. Maybe before.

And maybe he should just keep his distance. Besides, she would surely be in church on Sunday.

Except, she wasn't in church on Sunday. Meredith was there, and when Dean asked about Ann, Meredith said, "She insisted on staying home with Dad this week."

Yes, of course she did, Dean thought, *because*

she knew I'd be here. Smiling, he said, "I hope that means Wes is improved."

"Much," Meredith confirmed. "He's still weak, of course, and his immune system is increasingly compromised, but at least his nausea is gone. That will only last until his next chemotherapy session, but for now he feels better."

"Glad to hear it," Dean said, and he meant it. He lifted a hand to the back of his head and asked, "Would you happen to know if Ann's had a chance to look over my books? She was going to help me with a business plan."

Meredith shrugged. "Sorry. I couldn't say. She's spent a lot of time in the office lately, though. Maybe that's what's keeping her so busy. Should I tell her you asked?"

Shaking his head, Dean backed away. "Naw. I'll give her a couple more days. Thanks, though. Do give my best to Wes." He left Meredith nodding.

Certain that Ann was avoiding him, Dean stayed away from the ranch house on Monday, but by Tuesday evening, though tired to the bone, he couldn't bear it anymore. Telling himself that the longer this went on, the more awkward their next meeting would be, he cleaned up, left Donovan with his grandmother and drove back to the Straight Arrow.

Meredith answered the door, smiling warmly.

Dean pulled his hat and nodded in greeting but didn't beat around the bush.

"Ann here?"

Her smile seemed to fade slightly. "Sure. I'll go up and get her. Meanwhile, will you see Dad? He's feeling like a caged tiger these days."

"Be glad to."

Meredith waved him inside, took his hat, hung it on a peg on the wall and pointed toward the living room as she started up the stairs, calling out, "Dean is here, Dad."

Wes brought his recliner into its upright position and stood, turning to face Dean. He appeared much improved, maybe even a little heavier, as if his skin wasn't quite as loose over his bones. "Hey, there, Dean Paul. How's it going?"

"Harvest is coming along fine," Dean answered carefully, walking into the room.

"I'd shake your hand, but I'm not supposed to," Wes said cheerfully. "They're afraid some common old bug will get me before the cancer can."

"Lots of folks are praying healing and protection on you," Dean told him, "against old bugs, new bugs, cancer and everything else."

"And I appreciate it," Wes said with a broad smile. "Appreciate it and count on it. Now, take a seat." As Dean moved toward the sofa, Wes added, "I want to know what's going on with Ann."

Dean paused, halfway between the sofa and standing. Before he could formulate any sort of reply, Ann spoke from the shadows at the foot of the stairs.

"I keep telling you, Dad, nothing's going on. Rex just has me buried with work, and I'm worried about you. Am I not allowed to worry about you?"

"Yes, sugar, you're allowed to worry about me," Wes conceded. "You're not allowed to worry yourself sick."

"*I'm* not sick," Ann snapped, already turning toward the office door across the foyer. "In here, if you please, Dean. Let's get to it."

Glancing at Wes, who sighed deeply, Dean straightened and followed Ann into the office. What he saw there shocked him. She had dark rings around her eyes, wore no makeup at all and appeared haggard, as if she hadn't slept in days. Her hair had been swept up into a messy ponytail, and her faded, rumpled T-shirt looked like something left over from her high school days. Dean had never seen her so unkempt. Worse, she appeared dull, lifeless, as if she cared for nothing and no one.

"Your annual income is more than adequate," she stated flatly, standing behind the desk and flipping through some stapled papers. "You pay too much for insurance and way too much in taxes. Fire whoever is doing your taxes for you."

"That would be me," Dean noted flippantly, trying to inject a little humor into the moment.

She glanced up at that, shrugged and said, "You don't know what you're doing. Pay someone who does. You'll save money." With that, she tossed the papers at him.

"That's it?" he asked, both surprised and dismayed.

"No. There are phone apps to keep track of your mileage, fuel costs and so forth." She pulled a sheet from another pile and slung it across the desk. "I made a list for you."

He ignored the list and reached for her hand. "Ann, what's wrong?"

Jerking free of him, she turned her back and pulled a folder from a shelf. "Here's my recommendation, a step-by-step plan for realigning your budget, capitalizing and growing your business." She plopped the folder onto the desk, saying, "Study it. Hire a CPA. Get with Rex after he comes home. He'll steer you to the right bank and—"

"Jolly," Dean interrupted softly. "Talk to me. Please."

"I *am*," she snapped, frowning.

"Forget the business stuff," he began.

"Business is my thing!" Ann insisted hotly. Leaning her palms flat against the desktop. "Business is what I'm best at, management especially. Some people would go to great lengths, *very* great lengths, to secure my advice and expertise." Straightening, she folded her arms and glared at him.

He didn't know how or why, but he was suddenly standing on very shaky ground here. Drawing in a steadying breath through his nostrils, he spoke calmly.

"I'm sure that's true, and I appreciate everything you've said and done. Truly I do."

Despite her outburst, she shrugged as if it made no difference to her one way or another. Dean folded the paper and stashed it inside the folder, which he tucked under his arm, thinking furiously. Something was very wrong here, but he didn't have a clue what it might be. He turned reluctantly toward the door. Then inspiration struck, and he turned back again.

"You missed church on Sunday. Maybe you'd like to go to prayer meeting with me tomorrow night." Ann blinked at him before shaking her head. "Why not?"

Don't say that kiss. Don't say that kiss. Please, God, don't let her say it's because of that kiss.

She lifted her chin, but her eyes remained downcast. "I don't have anything to wear."

He raked his gaze over her. "That's an absurd reason."

She opened her mouth as if she would argue, but he didn't give her the chance.

"Don't you feel moved to pray for your father's health? When was the last time you joined with a group of others in focused prayer?" She stared at him for several seconds, robbing herself of any opportunity to refuse. "I'll pick you up at six thirty," he said, turning to open the door. He walked out before she could speak again, pulling the door closed firmly behind him.

He spent the rest of the night and almost the entirety of the next day praying that she wouldn't close the door in his face when he came for her.

To his immense relief, Ann stepped through the front door of the ranch house the next evening before he even got to the porch. Dressed in a flared skirt and familiar lace T-shirt, with no makeup other than some subtly colored lip gloss, her long, vibrant hair hanging straight past her shoulders, she looked like a sixteen-year-old in her mom's high heels.

He fell for her all over again, just like the chubby, awkward thirteen-year-old he'd been the first time he'd laid eyes on her in the dugout at the War Bonnet High School baseball field. She hadn't even known he was alive back then. To her, he was just some kid who delivered a fresh ball to the ump after she smashed one over the fence or who darted out and snatched up her bat after she tossed it aside to run the bases. To him, she'd been as near perfect as a girl could get.

One of them had changed. But not enough. She was still the girl who could knock the ball out of the park, while he had moved on from ball boy to…barely-getting-by dad.

He wouldn't trade Donovan for a college degree or a career, but he couldn't help wanting to be more for her, for a chance with her. Not that he'd ever have such a chance. If he could help her somehow, though, that would be enough. Whatever had gone wrong for her, if he could find a way to help that would be enough. It had to be.

Smiling, he said, "Love your hair like that."

Lifting a hand to her side part self-consciously, she actually seemed shocked, but all she said was, "Shouldn't we go?"

Dean had lots of practice at hiding disappointment. Keeping his smile in place took hardly any effort at all. "Right. Let's move."

He lifted an arm, and she stepped down off the porch onto the path, striding quickly toward the truck parked at the side of the road, so quickly that she stayed a half step ahead of him. He had to rush past her and leap across the ditch to get the passenger door for her. She slid up into the seat without even glancing at him.

Sighing, he jogged around and got in behind the steering wheel, started up the truck, made the U-turn and headed toward the church.

Just as he turned the dually into the parking lot of Countryside Church, he glanced down and saw her left hand dangling off the armrest. Her very naked left hand.

Before he could think, he blurted, "Where's your ring?"

She turned dull eyes on him then looked away again, moving her hand to her lap. "Probably in Dallas by now."

He quickly pulled the truck into a parking space, his mind abuzz with questions. Had she broken her engagement? Was that what lay behind her downcast mood of late? Was she heartbroken? Confused? Uncertain what or who she wanted? Or all of the above?

Before he could ask any of those questions, she'd bailed out of the truck and started across the graveled lot. His heart thudding, Dean threw the transmission into park, killed the engine and went after her, catching up within steps. Impulsively, he slipped an arm across her shoulders. She didn't even break stride, giving him no reaction at all. Uncertain what to do next—she could be having the ring cleaned, after all—he decided, perhaps cravenly, to go with small talk.

"School starts in exactly one week. Can you

believe it? We haven't even hit the middle of August yet, and school is about to start." She nodded but said nothing. "I don't mind admitting that I'm not looking forward to it," he went on. "My little boy's growing up, and it's tough to take."

As if that had penetrated her blankness, she stopped and turned a surprisingly endearing look on him. "You're a good father, Dean." A hint of a smile curved one corner of her mouth. "A lousy businessman but a good father."

Relieved to see something like real emotion in her, and anxious to further lighten her mood, he chuckled. "Well, I've got you to help me with the business part, and things like tonight help with the father part. You know, I never really prayed until Donovan came into my life," he admitted. "Then suddenly I had this helpless, amazing, *tiny* person to take care of. Scared the fool out of me. I knew I'd die to protect him but that I *couldn't* always. So I started praying, and now sometimes I feel like that's all I do."

Nodding pensively, Ann threaded her fingers through his. "I can see how that might be. But Donovan's going to be fine. You're giving him everything he needs to get through life."

"Like your parents did for you," Dean pointed out subtly.

She blinked up at him.

Just then, one of the deacons, a middle-aged man, hurried past them and pushed open the glass double door, holding it wide. "Coming in?"

Dean hadn't exactly been a regular at mid-week prayer meeting in a while, especially since the children's choir director had resigned to have a baby. With the children's program on hold, Dean usually stayed home with Donovan so Grandma Betty could come to the meeting, but tonight they had switched so he could bring Ann with him.

"Yes, thank you," he called to the deacon, stepping out again, Ann's hand firmly clasped in his.

Together they walked into the building. The place felt oddly quiet, serene, even, though Dean knew from the number of cars in the parking lot that dozens of people had to be inside. He was glad that each and every one had come, but tonight the person he cared about most was the woman at his side, holding his hand.

He was beginning to think that he would always want her at his side, always need her to hold his hand.

Simply holding hands with someone should not have been so comforting, but Ann had never been so shaken, and unlike most women, she was truly lousy at sharing her feelings. She'd known Jordan for years before she'd told him how an overheard conversation had driven her into hotel management. And he had used that knowledge to try to break her bond with her family and keep her on the job—when, now that she thought about it, the job was really all she had to hold on to.

She told herself that latching on to Dean would be foolish in the extreme because eventually she must go back to her job in Dallas. At first she'd thought otherwise, that when her engagement ended, her job would also, but then she'd checked online for comparable job openings, and everything she'd found would take her even farther away from her dad and the rest of the family than Dallas.

Strangely, it wasn't so much that she wanted to go back to the Dallas job. Her life in Dallas seemed sterile and lonely now. Over these last few weeks, she'd gotten used to sharing a home with her father and sister again. Having company, sitting down to meals together, enjoying real conversations, even trading those small, casual expressions of affection—a touch, a kiss on the cheek, a quick hug—those things all made life so much more...worthwhile. She just didn't know what she'd do with herself on a productive, day-to-day basis if she *didn't* go back to her job at Luxury Hotels, Inc.

Nevertheless, Rex, Callie and baby Bodie would be home soon, and Rex would once again pick up the reins of the Straight Arrow operation, not that he'd ever completely relinquished them. Ann feared that she would feel displaced and in the way once he stepped back into his managerial role.

On the other hand, in only a few more days her dad would return to the hospital in Oklahoma City for more chemotherapy; it wouldn't be the last, and she hated the idea of not being here for him as he fought this disease. Seeing him so ill after the chemo infusions broke her heart, but how could she walk away while he battled for his very life?

Beneath the shock of Jordan's lies, she felt lost and uncertain. She'd been able to keep panic at bay with work and a stoic refusal to face the future. Now that Dean had noticed she wasn't wearing her ring, suddenly Jordan was behind her, and the future stared her in the face. The time had come to begin making plans.

During the meeting, she asked for her father's healing and comfort, but her private, unspoken prayer sought clear, obvious direction for her life. Try as she might, though, she couldn't see her way forward. Where should she go? What should she do? For what job should she apply? She had only questions, no answers.

Throughout it all, Dean held her hand in his He became her anchor in the rocky sea of uncertainty that had become her life.

As the meeting progressed, however, and those around her lifted their voices in prayer often for her father, Ann's strength began to return. She didn't know what she was going to do but she began to feel that she could figure it ou in time. In too many ways, she still felt at sea but the storm began to calm, and she started to believe that she would make it to land, though just where she might wash up she couldn't quite imagine yet.

By the end of the evening, she was very glac that she had come, though she almost hadn't. In fact, she couldn't really say why she *had* come At 6:00 p.m. she'd been determined to tell Dear to get lost, and then suddenly she'd wondered what she had to lose by going with him. After running upstairs to trade her jeans for a skirt and her boots for shoes, she'd told Meredith that she was going out for a while and had been sitting on the porch when he'd arrived at thirty minutes past the hour. She hadn't analyzed why she'd changed her mind; she'd just done it.

Maybe it was because Dean somehow made her feel safe and appreciated, the *real* her, the one so few people actually knew.

As they walked back to the dually after the

prayer meeting, Dean slid his arm about her shoulders again. His support felt so good that she couldn't help leaning into him just a bit. He opened the passenger door for her and held her hand as she stepped up into the truck. Settling behind the steering wheel a few seconds later, he smiled at her.

The silence felt easy and calm as they drove back to the ranch. When they got there, rather than pull to the very edge of the road as he usually did, he stopped the wide-bed truck right in the middle. Then he got out and came around to open the door for her. She waited, appreciating the gentlemanly gesture.

"Thank you," she said simply.

"You're welcome," he responded, but when she turned toward the house, he caught her by the left hand, bringing her to a halt. "Why did you send back the ring?" he asked softly, enunciating each word carefully.

She didn't have the energy or the will to tell him the whole story, so she finally came out with, "It's not going to work out between me and Jordan."

Dean pressed his thumb over the vacant space on her ring finger. "You're breaking up with him?" She nodded, and then Dean was pulling her to him. "Good."

He wrapped his arms around her, dipped his head and kissed her.

Her head swimming, she pulled back enough to ask, "Is that all you have to say?"

Step by step, he backed her against the truck, asking, "What do you want me to say? That it's the best news I've heard in ages? Because it is."

Then he was kissing her again, and it was so difficult to think when he was kissing her. She tried to be sensible, though. Even as her arms slid up around his neck, she broke away again, trying to clear her brain.

"Dean," she said desperately, "I'm not sure I'm cut out for what you may have in mind."

"Hush," he told her, pressing a fingertip to her lips. "This is all I have in mind at the moment. I've waited years for this, longer than you know." He bowed his head to hers, whispering, "I've prayed for this."

He drew her like metal to magnet, so that he was no longer kissing her. She was kissing him.

By the time he stopped and said that he had to get home to Donovan, she could barely kiss him for grinning. Pushing away from her, he took several deep breaths, carefully stood her a safe distance away from the fender, then reluctantly trudged around to the driver's door and opened it then paused to shake his head at her.

"Am I feminine?" he parroted in a wry, silly

voice. "That has to be one of the stupidest questions ever asked." He shook his head again before getting into the truck and slamming the door. Starting the engine, he gave her a hard look. Then he grinned and began backing toward the drive at the rear of the house, where he could turn the truck around.

Ann laughed, practically dancing on air as she strolled through the trees to the front door.

Chapter Eleven

Dancing on air.

That was how Dean felt for all of twenty-four hours. He couldn't stop smiling, and he couldn't seem to just walk anywhere. When he went down for breakfast on Thursday morning, he expected Grandma to ask why he was so happy. He didn't know what he was going to tell her.

Nothing was settled between him and Ann. She'd ended her engagement with that Jordan Teel character, and she'd kissed him, Dean, but that was all that had happened. So far.

That didn't keep Dean from dreaming and planning. He told himself that with her business know-how and his hard work, they could really build something together. He hadn't looked at her business plan yet, but when he realigned his budget, surely he could work in a reasonable payment on an engagement ring. Maybe he'd never be able to afford a diamond the size of that thing she'd taken off, but then size couldn't matter as much as the man who offered it. Could it?

All Dean really knew about Jordan Teel was what he'd seen at Rex's wedding: an older man who spent a lot of money on clothes. Apparently Teel hadn't recognized Ann's uncertainty about her feminine appeal. Dean neither knew nor cared why she had confided in him about that, but he thanked God that she had. He would happily reassure her on that score at any time, not that he particularly wanted to tell his grandmother that.

Thankfully, as she placed his eggs before him, Betty asked only, "How was prayer meeting last night?"

"Good," he answered, taking up his fork and glancing at her. "I think it did Ann a lot of good."

Betty patted him on the shoulder as she headed back to the stove. "Prayer always does."

And that was it. Donovan was too busy smearing jelly on his toast to pay attention to anything the adults had to say. Dean smiled and ate his eggs.

Half an hour later the dually bumped over the pipes that Rex had laid out to bridge the ditch into the sorghum field, where Ann sat on the fender of her dad's truck, wearing running clothes and smiling broadly. The combine sat far

in the distance, across already harvested acres
but Dean brought the dually to a halt. Only Donovan's presence kept Dean from jumping out
sweeping Ann into his arms and kissing them
both stupid.

"I won't be long," Dean said to his son and hi
dog, opening his door and getting out.

He couldn't keep the smile off his face as he
strolled over the uneven ground to greet her
"Good morning."

She nodded, her ponytail bouncing, and said
"Thought I'd come out to see how far you've
gotten." Squinting across the field, she added
"Dad's heading back to the city for another treat
ment, and he's wondering when you'll be done
I wanted to reassure him before he goes."

"We're just about done here," Dean told her
"I'll be delivering the last of this to storage before next week."

"That soon?"

"Mmm-hmm." He pointed to the trailers al
ready loaded with the rich fodder. "Tell him no
to worry. We're making good headway."

"That will make him feel better, I'm sure."

"When will he get back home?" Dean asked

"Not sure," she answered, shaking her head
"Meri says that a lot depends on how he han
dles things at this stage." Ann sighed, adding
"I can't shake the feeling that I should go with

them. She had a hard time getting him home by herself last time. Would it be a hardship for you if I wasn't here to sign checks for a few days?"

Dean shook his head. "I don't have any help to pay right now. I can manage until you get back. Go if you need to."

She looked off to the east then, saying, "I'd forgotten how pretty the sunrise is out here."

"Not as pretty as you," he said, smoothing an imaginary tendril of hair away from her cheek.

Glancing down, she tilted her head just enough to maintain brief contact with his hand. "You don't have to say that."

"I've always thought you were the most beautiful girl in War Bonnet."

Pegging him with those sky eyes of hers, she smiled slightly. "You really mean that, don't you?"

"With all my heart."

Her smile grew, and she looked down at her hands, asking, "Have you had a chance to look at the business plan I drew up for you?"

"Not yet, but I will. Tonight, hopefully."

Nodding, she hopped off the fender and moved toward the driver's door. "Okay." She opened the door and got inside the truck. He reached out and caught the edge of it before she could pull it closed.

"Ann."

"Yeah?"

"I don't know why you broke up with tha Dallas guy, but if he doesn't fight for you, he' an idiot."

Sadness tinged her smile, and she shook he head. "I'm the idiot," she told him, "but at leas I found out in time."

Dean crouched behind the open door, bring ing his gaze level with hers. "Then he doesn' deserve you."

She laughed and rolled her eyes. "Right. I'n Jolly Billings, the best slugger ever to come ou of War Bonnet High."

"And don't you forget it," he told her with grin, coming to his feet and at the same time bending at the waist so he could kiss her fore head.

Still laughing, she started the engine. He backed away and closed the truck door.

"Go or stay, just take care," he told her throug the open window.

"Say a prayer for us."

"Several," he promised.

She blew him a kiss before starting the truc forward.

Dancing on air, even as he trudged back t his own vehicle, he watched her drive out of th field and go on her way.

Then that evening he sat down to study he

business plan. The crash back to earth came as a very painful jolt indeed.

He tore the thing apart, came at it from every angle he could find, but no matter how he looked at it, her plan could not possibly work without a serious injection of capital to fund a real expansion of his business. Where he was supposed to get that kind of money, he didn't know, couldn't even imagine. Even if he took a mortgage out on the house and remaining acreage, the resulting funds would not do what Ann suggested needed to be done. As things stood, he *might* be able to establish a modest line of credit, but that was about it.

Certainly if he could find a way to get his hands on the capital that Ann believed he required, her number projections looked great, but he could see no way to come up with that much cash. Or *any* cash, really, not if he intended to feed, clothe, house and transport his son, never mind himself.

He felt sick. Reality had just crashed his dreams. He thought of the plans he'd been forming in the back of his mind, some of which had hovered there for a decade or more, never seeing the light of day until just recently. Only lately had he even dared to actually *think* these things, let alone pray about them.

Now it was as if God had just told him in no uncertain terms that Ann was not for him.

Dean had traded a college degree and a career for fatherhood, the rewards of which were too numerous to count. He should be happy with that. He would have to be happy with that. It was all he could afford, all he'd ever be able to afford, no matter how hard he worked.

Maybe, after Grandma died—he prayed that wouldn't be soon, not before Donovan was grown and on his own—Dean could sell the house and remaining land, buy more equipment and a little trailer to live in. He could live on the move, following the work, and lay up a tidy sum that way then retire secure. That was no way of life for a family man, though. That was a single man's solution.

So obviously Dean was meant to be a single man.

He stopped sneaking peeks at engagement rings on the internet and concentrated on just getting through, hour by hour. Having learned that the key to overcoming self-pity was gratitude, Dean made a concerted effort to thank God for His every blessing, starting with the red headed, freckle-faced boy who called him Dad.

Sadly, he couldn't help wondering how long it would be before he stopped seeing Ann every time he looked at his son now. Deflated and de pressed, he finished the sorghum harvest and delivered it, truckload after truckload, glad that Ann did not put in another appearance. He assumed that she'd gone to Oklahoma City with her father and sister, but he carried his statement to the house that Friday evening as usual, intending to wedge it between the casing and the edge of the front door. He didn't even make it across the porch before the door opened, however, and Callie, Rex's wife, smiled at him, her little daughter on her hip.

"Dean Paul! Hello."

"You're back," he said stupidly, his stomach dropping all the way to his toes.

She nodded her shaggy blond head, and Bodie, her baby girl, copied her. "We just got in. Rex was going to come out to see you, but you beat him to it. He's in the office looking for the checkbook. Go on in."

Dean muttered his thanks as he followed her into the foyer, but all he could think was that Ann would surely be heading back to Dallas now. It shouldn't matter, but somehow it did.

"Where's Donovan?" Callie asked. "I have some cookies for him."

"Oh, he's already belted into his safety seat in the truck," Dean told her.

"Well, you can take them to him," Callie said.

"They're already bagged up, left over from our trip. I'll just go get them while you talk to Rex."

"That's very kind," Dean managed, kneading his work cap and painfully aware that he hadn't yet made his feet budge in the direction of the office.

She hurried away, and he faced that office door, which stood open, just waiting for him to enter. Dean liked Rex; he really did, but having him home felt like the death knell to every hope and dream Dean had ever nurtured.

"In some ways, I feel like my dreams have been dashed," Ann admitted, "and in others I feel as if I'm just now waking up to reality."

Her father reached out, his hand still surprisingly heavy and strong, despite the web of hoses trailing it, and patted her knee. "I'm glad you sent back the ring," he told her, "and I think you were wise to do it without explanation. I hope you'll tender your resignation the same way, but that's for you to decide."

Sighing, Ann shrugged. She didn't know why she'd waited until now to tell her father about her broken engagement. Something about hospital rooms seemed to invite confidences. Of course, she hadn't told him all of it, just that she'd mistakenly left the line open after a telephone call very early one morning and overheard Jordan telling another woman that marrying Ann was nothing more than a career move on his part.

"He's called, but I haven't answered. The thing is, I don't know what I'll do if I don't go back to LHI," she confessed gloomily.

"What do you want to do?" her dad asked, but she dared not answer that question. She wasn't quite ready to lay herself *that* bare.

It was too soon. A woman didn't just dump her fiancé and jump to another man. Not that doing so was even an option. Dean hadn't said anything about a relationship with her. All they'd done was kiss. Maybe if she could stick around long enough, things would develop into something serious between them.

Wes cleared his throat. "Maybe I should ask *who* you want."

Ann stared at him, wide-eyed. "Am I that obvious?"

Wes chuckled. "You're both that obvious."

Groaning, Ann squeezed her eyes shut. "Now, don't get the wrong idea. Dean had nothing to do with me breaking my engagement. Nothing happened between us until I ended things with Jordan."

Her father's pale blue gaze brightened. "So something did happen between you and Dean, then."

"Nothing of any significance," she stated

flatly. Unless you called having your world rocked significant.

Grinning, Wes said, "Yes, I can see that. You know, sugar, there's nothing wrong with a woman going after what she wants. Dean is a good man. I'd venture to say there are few to none better."

As if she had to be told that. Not that Dean was perfect by any means.

"He has less education than me."

"So? Most likely he could finish his degree online these days. If he wanted to. I'm not sure it makes any difference. Dean's not the sort to work for anyone but himself."

That was true, and she certainly couldn't fault him for it. But was he flexible enough to accept help when it was offered? She could help him. She knew that she could. When she'd gone over his books, she'd seen the possibilities right away, and she hadn't even been thinking about a partnership between the two of them then.

That was what she wanted with a man, a true partnership, in which each of them brought unique talents and abilities to the joining that made the pair of them together stronger and more successful than either of them could be alone. The saddest part about her and Jordan and LHI was simply that if Jordan and Marshal had sat her down and explained that with her at Jordan's side, he would soon become a vice president of the company, she would have happily and proudly hotfooted it back to Dallas as the earliest opportunity. They hadn't done it that way for one reason: It had never occurred to them. It had never occurred to them to discuss that possibility with her because Jordan did not love or value her. To him, she was a means to an end and nothing more. To Dean she was a woman whom he found attractive, but was that it?

She desperately wanted to believe that Dean saw—and wanted—the real her, the whole her, but how much of that was genuine feeling and how much was simple attraction?

"He lives with his grandmother," she said, tipping her nose into the air.

"Actually," Wes drawled, pressing his head back into his pillow, "if you want to get technical about it, she lives with him. Milburn set up a trust when he became ill, leaving everything to Dean, with Betty and her daughter, Deana Kay Wilton, as executors until Dean turned eighteen. That's how Dean was able to sell off the land to buy farming equipment and go into business for himself after Donovan was born."

"I wonder what Betty thought about him selling off the land," Ann murmured, trying to put herself in Betty Pryor's place.

"Oh, she was all for it," Wes informed Ann.

"She, Deana and Dean Paul came to talk to me about it. Stuart Crowsen had offered him a loan, but I thought the terms were…dangerous."

"You advised him to sell rather than borrow."

"I did. But only after we prayed about it first."

Ann felt her chin quiver at the thought of her father and Dean, who couldn't have been more than twenty at the time, sitting down together to pray.

I never really prayed until Donovan came into my life…now sometimes I feel like that's all I do.

"He's younger than me," Ann pointed out softly.

Wes chuckled. "If Dean Paul Pryor isn't a man fully grown, I'd like to know what your definition for a real adult male is."

Ann had to smile. "He's stretched out on this bed here."

"Aw, sugar."

"I have to say," Ann went on carefully, "Dean measures up pretty well. And I never thought I'd say that about any man, really." She realized with a shock that she'd just accepted at some point that no man would ever measure up to her dad. She'd been wrong about that, and because she'd been wrong, she'd been willing to settle for less than she should have.

Wes's eyes filled with tears. Reaching out, he caught his hand against the back of her head and pulled her to him for a hug that set off alarms all around the room.

Laughing and dashing away her own tears, Ann settled back into her chair to await the nurses about to burst into the room.

"Well," Wes demanded, "what are you doing sitting around here? You should be back in War Bonnet."

"You know that Meredith needs my help on the trip home," Ann replied diplomatically.

"You aren't needed until then, though," Wes told her as a pair of nurses swept through the door. They fluttered around adjusting intravenous tubes and resetting machines while he argued. "The road runs both ways, you know. Go home. Come back to get us."

"I can't take Meri's car and leave her stranded," Ann protested, but she was already out of her chair and staring at the door.

"You never heard of car rental?"

Her heart beating swiftly, Ann dropped a kiss onto her father's forehead. "I love you, Dad."

"I love you, too," he rumbled, "and I'm pretty fond of that redheaded kid who keeps eating my cookies."

Laughing, Ann practically flew from the room.

Getting out of Oklahoma City took considerably more time than Ann expected, so the hour was later than she'd have liked when she pulled her sister's little car to a stop beneath the old tree behind the ranch house on Saturday evening. They'd arranged a rental for Meredith to drive, and then Ann had needed to repack, eat, find an ATM to make sure she had cash, fill up the gas tank, call Rex to let him know she was on her way home...

When she came through the back door, the house was quiet and dark except for the distant hum and flicker of the television in the living room. Aware that her little niece would be sleeping, Ann carried her suitcase through the mudroom, past the rear bath that opened into both the hall and her father's room, through the kitchen and up the back stairs. A glimpse into the living room showed her two figures sitting close together on the leather sofa.

Ann considered calling out to let her brother and sister-in-law know that she was there, but she didn't want to wake the baby. Instead, she slipped up the stairs and dropped her bags in her room then crept back down to the kitchen where she flipped on a light, went to the sink and ran a glass of water, clinking dishes and bumping into chairs. Basically, she did everything she could think of to signal her presence without waking baby Bodie.

When she walked into the living room, Rex and Callie looked over at her.

"How was your trip?" Rex asked.

"Boring," she answered drily, plopping down into her father's recliner. "I hate driving alone."

"Then why did you?" Rex asked.

"I was in the way at the hospital," she said, leaning back in the chair. "And Meri's cat's lousy company."

He rolled his eyes. "I can't stay at Meri's apartment with that cat, either."

"I thought maybe I could be of more use here." She plucked at a knotted thread in the denim of her jeans. "How's the sorghum going?"

"It's done," Rex told her easily, draping his arm around his wife's shoulders. "Dean delivered the last of it yesterday evening."

"That's it?" she blurted, feeling stung. She'd known that it would be soon, but she'd thought it would happen Monday maybe.

Rex nodded, playing with a tendril of Callie's short, wispy hair. "Good harvest. And he did a great job with the mixing station. He actually moved the footprint slightly, but it works better this way. He would know, of course, how best to place it so you can back a pickup bed right up to the mixing pan."

Ann hummed in agreement, but all she could think was that Dean wouldn't be coming back to the ranch, not until planting time, anyway. Callie laid her head on Rex's shoulder, and he bent his head to whisper into her ear. She nodded, and they began rising from the sofa. A shaft of envy speared straight through Ann.

"Guess we'll call it a night, sis. Glad you made it home safe. See you in the morning."

Nodding, she reminded herself that they were deliriously in love and basically still honeymooning, but it did no good. As they left the room, arm in arm, she knew with sudden, shocking clarity that she wanted exactly what they had, that calm, sure, complimentary partnership underpinned with a deep abiding love, an unmistakable physical attraction and a shared, unshakeable faith. It seemed so simple, really—and all-encompassing.

Everything. It was everything.

Suddenly what she'd had—even what she'd *thought* she'd had—with Jordan seemed small, shabby and artificial. She couldn't believe that she'd been willing to settle for what he'd offered, what she'd actually thought she wanted. For the first time she realized how truly great a fool she had been.

Jordan, she realized, could not be blamed for her shallow foolishness, only for taking advantage of it. No, this was all on her. She'd let her insecurities drive her away from what was most dear in her life and had clung to her career and intellectual abilities for redemption, rather than her faith. Perhaps she'd even been angry with God for making her less than what she'd imagined she should be, when that had never been the case. She'd allowed one unimportant person's opinion to color her entire life and determine her future, even her career path, and she'd almost let it lead her to commit a great folly in marrying the wrong man.

Well, no more.

She told God how sorry she was, and then, as she turned off the TV and the lights and climbed the stairs, she began to pray for courage.

Chapter Twelve

Dean knew the moment that Ann Billings entered the sanctuary. He'd have known even if heads hadn't turned, which had prompted his to turn, as well. Something in the air changed when Ann came around. He'd felt it long, long ago, a specific electrical charge as unique to Ann as the smell of her skin, the color of her hair, the taste of her lips. That electricity shimmered through him even as his head turned and his torso twisted, his gaze unerringly targeting the tall, elegantly beautiful woman strutting down the aisle in lemon-yellow shoes with ridiculously tall heels.

The shoes matched the tank top that she wore beneath the slender, charcoal-gray suit that screamed money and class to everyone in the room. The straight skirt stopped demurely at her knees, and the neatly tailored jacket nipped in at the waist in a decidedly feminine fashion. She'd caught her long, vibrant hair in a neat bun at the nape of her neck, allowing long tendrils to frame a face made up with the barest touch of rosy lipstick and dark mascara.

She looked like a queen, certainly not a farmer's wife. Most especially not the wife of a farmer without a farm of his own.

He didn't have the courage to approach her, but he didn't have the strength to ignore her, either. Feeling beaten by the sheer, unreachable beauty of her, Dean turned away, pierced to the core, and prayed that she'd keep her distance. He didn't think he could bear being around her; he didn't think he could resist if she pressed.

Not a word of the service stuck in his mind. It all flowed right through his thoughts like so much flotsam in a stream. He tried to seize on the theme of the sermon, to lose himself in worship, to feel the presence of the Holy Spirit as he had so often in the past, but all he could feel, all he could think about, all he could focus upon was Ann and the deep, yawning sense of loss that he felt.

Beside him, his grandmother shifted uneasily. She had sensed that all was not well with him. He'd blamed the pending start of the school year in just three days' time, but he wasn't sure that Betty bought it. Even Donovan had felt his father's disquiet. The boy had climbed onto Dean's lap the previous evening for tickles and hugs, something he hadn't done in quite a while. He was such a big boy that he had outgrown Dean's lap, and his laughter, while bright and warming, had seemed just a little forced. Dean had felt grateful but not comforted.

He missed her. He would always miss her, but everything—including that dazzling suit she wore today—said that she didn't belong with him. Agonizing internally, he opened his Bible to Romans, his favorite book, and thumbed through the pages until his gaze fell on the second verse of the twelfth chapter.

Do not conform to the pattern of this world, but be transformed by the renewing of your mind. Then you will be able to test and approve what God's will is—His good, pleasing and perfect will.

The pattern of the world. Did that mean Dean should disregard all these signs he thought he saw, everything that seemed to tell him that he and Ann couldn't work? Or was that so much wishful thinking on his part? He shook his head, knowing that he couldn't trust himself to divine anything correctly. His desire got in the way. So much for renewing his mind.

He flipped a few pages over and came to the eighth chapter. Verse twenty-seven said, *And He*

Who searches our hearts knows the mind of the Spirit, because the Spirit intercedes for God's people in accordance with the will of God.

Dean closed his eyes and simply thought, *Intercede for me, Lord. I don't know what to say or do except...thank You.*

After the service he went straight out the side door to get Donovan. As usual, the boy bubbled over with what he'd learned that morning, waving around his coloring papers and story folder. Dean nodded and listened, half hearing as he shepherded his son back to the sanctuary. There he found his grandmother and Ann cozily chatting amongst a knot of three or four other women.

Ann's gaze zipped unerringly to meet his. Then suddenly Donovan ran across the emptying sanctuary to throw himself at her.

"Ann! You're back!"

She went down on her knees to greet him, accepting his hug with a wide smile. "Hello, Donovan!"

"You can come, then," he declared. "Dad said you might not be back in time, but you are, so you can come for the first day of school!"

Ann glanced up at Dean then smiled apologetically at his son. "I can't promise, Donovan. I'm sorry. I may have to go back before Wednesday."

"Awwww." Donovan stepped away, slapping his hands against his thighs in disappointment

"My father will be very ill when he gets out of the hospital," Ann explained gently. "My sister can't drive and take care of him, too. I have to go help. But it may not be on Wednesday. I just don't know yet."

"The hospital is in Oklahoma City," Dean said, gathering Donovan against him. He knew just how the boy felt, but nothing could be done about this. "You've been to the city. You remember, don't you?"

Donovan nodded. "It's a long way," he whispered huskily.

"Perhaps Ann would like to join us for Sunday dinner," Betty suggested, "just in case she's not able to be here on Wednesday."

Dean felt as if he'd received a blow to the gut, but Donovan looked up with a grin. "Okay! We got kittens in the barn."

Ann's eyebrows jumped. "Kittens?"

"Yeah, four of them," Donovan reported happily, "but we can't keep 'em all."

Ann groaned and looked at Dean. "You won't tell Meri, will you? She's insane for cats."

He couldn't help but smile. His heart was cracking into pieces, but she could still make him smile. "Not a word," he solemnly pledged

"I have to go home and change," Ann said, cupping Donovan's chin in her hand.

Betty chuckled. "We'll see you shortly."

"Yes, and thank you."

She looked Dean straight in the eye then, as if willing him to repeat his grandmother's invitation—or rescind it. He could do nothing more than nod and usher his son up the aisle after his rapidly retreating grandmother.

He didn't have the courage to welcome Ann or the strength to rebuff her.

Intercede for me. Intercede for me. Oh, please, Lord, intercede for me...

Dean hadn't exactly welcomed her at church that morning. Ann had to wonder if he regretted the kisses they'd shared. Maybe he feared that she had developed expectations. She had not—unless wishes were expectations.

After changing her clothes, Ann thought about calling the Pryors to cancel, using the excuse that Callie had prepared a special dinner without her knowledge, which was true. But then every meal Callie prepared seemed to be special, and both Callie and Rex encouraged her to go. Because Rex happened to be on the phone with their father at the time, Wes got in on the act, asking to speak to Ann himself.

"So, Sunday dinner with the Pryors, huh? Well, that's a tonic to a sick man."

Now, how could she argue with that, especially as he sounded sick? She brightened her chatter mentioning that Donovan was campaigning to get her to accompany him and his father to his first day of kindergarten on Wednesday.

"Sounds like a fine idea," Wes said. "You should go."

"I'm just not sure about the timing," Ann countered. "I want to get back to the city before you need me."

"Kindergarten's only half-day. Right?"

"Yes."

"Then I see no problem," Wes said. "Take the boy to school. Pick him up again afterward. Then head up here. We can be home before bedtime. Unless that's too much driving for you in one day."

"No, no," Ann hastened to assure him. "That's fine. If you're sure."

"Works for me," Wes told her. "Now I need a nap."

Praying for her father's recovery and thanking God for his wisdom and generosity, Ann got in the truck and drove over to the Pryor place.

The old clapboard house, with its crisp white paint and unusual rounded porch that wrapped two sides of the first floor, seemed in pristine condition. Its pale green metal roof lent an air of gentility to the place, and the guttering, railings, flower beds and brick steps and walkways showed that a great deal of time and attention had been showered on the place over the decades. Easily a hundred years old, the inner windows still bore the wavy glass of the original era. Ann saw no chimney, only a smokestack. Three black rocking chairs, painted to match the trim around the many tall, narrow windows and doors, took pride of place on the porch, pots of colorful flowers spilling over around them.

A screen door at the end of the porch banged open, and Donovan and Digger came running out to greet her. She brought the truck to a stop on a neat patch of gravel hemmed in by railroad ties next to a large, white metal barn with three garage bays and several smaller doors. At the other end of the property she saw a white chicken coop with the same pale green metal roof as the house and barn. The whole tableau made a very sweet picture, especially given the tire swing and tree house in the big hickory shading the porch.

Dean came out of a door in the barn and lifted a hand in what seemed a halfhearted greeting. Ann slid out of the truck and smiled at him.

"Good news," he announced. "The cat's moved her kittens to some unknown location."

Ann chuckled. "You'll find them."

"I'm afraid so. Just not today."

"What a lovely place," she said then, glancing around. "Neat as a pin."

"Grandma's a great believer in orderliness," he divulged, ducking his head. "There's iced tea on the porch."

"Sounds nice."

Donovan hit her with a hug just as they rounded the rear end of the truck. "Come see my tree house!"

"I saw it when I drove up. Looks cool."

"Dad and me built it. Watch how you get up."

He ran to the tree and pulled on a rope. A ramp with rails slid down, braces dropping into place to keep it steady. Donovan half crawled, half ran up it, the dog on his heels.

Ann turned a delighted smile on Dean. "Wow! Did you do that?"

"He was pretty small when we built that," Dean said. "Too small to climb a ladder. We had to come up with some other way for him to get up there."

Donovan peeked over the wall of the tree house, calling, "Come on up!"

"Is it all right?"

"Sure. Go on."

She went up the ramp, finding it solid and steady, and crept through the open doorway or her hands and knees. Standing was possible in the center of the platform, but Dean had put a sloping roof on the thing so that it was sheltered from rain, and the outer walls were only tall enough for her if she stayed on her knees. She sat with her legs folded while Digger lolled in one corner and Donovan showed her his treasures: a huge acorn, a collection of cat-eye marbles in a tin box, several tiny cars, the skull of a squirrel and a trio of "super power" rings.

"I'm gonna sleep out here sometime," he announced, looking around with satisfaction. "Maybe this year."

She had the feeling that this event depended completely on his willingness to brave the night out-of-doors on his own.

"That sounds like fun," Ann said. "I remember the first time I slept outside. My brother and sister and I pitched a tent in our front yard and camped out. I never knew there were so many sounds outside at night."

"Dad and me, we've listened to 'em," Donovan confirmed sagely. Ann hid her smile, assuming that such listening might be the reason Donovan had not yet slept in his tree house.

The screen door on the house creaked again, and Betty appeared on the porch. "Dinner in fifteen minutes, everyone."

Ann went up on her knees and waved at Betty, calling down to her, "Anything I can do to help?"

"You and Dean can set the table, if you like," she called back, squinting up at the shadows beneath the tree.

"I'll take care of it," Dean said, starting toward the house.

Ann looked at Donovan, winked and said, "We better go."

"Come on, Digger," Donovan said, crawling to the exit. Ann followed.

It was easier to stand going down the ramp than it had been going up. She trailed Donovan across the thick grass to the brick walkway, with its lovely herringbone pattern. Dean waited for her at the top of the porch steps, a tall tumbler of cool iced tea in hand.

He nodded to Donovan, saying, "You go on in and wash up." Passing the cool glass to Ann, he added, "You just relax out here. Company shouldn't have to set the table."

"I don't mind," she told him, taking the glass.

"It's not too warm out here in the shade," he said, nodding toward one of the rocking chairs as she took a long drink of the cold, sweet tea.

"Oh, that's good," she gasped, feeling the icy coolness sweep through her. "Now, lead the way inside. I don't mind helping out at all."

Dean's jaw ground side to side, but he nodded

and turned toward the door. She didn't understand the issue, unless he *really* just didn't want her here. He opened the screen and turned the brass knob on the interior door, pushing it open for her. She stepped straight into a long, narrow, pearl-gray room with a potbellied stove in the far corner.

"Does that work?" Ann asked in surprise.

"It does, but it's a replica, a pellet stove. Grandma turned the original into a planter out back. That's where she grows her herbs."

"How ingenious!"

"You'd be surprised how much heat that pellet stove puts out," Dean told her. "It really knocks down the utility bills in the winter."

"Interesting. It looks right in here, too."

He grimaced. "It's all replicas in here because that's the style Grandma likes. The dining room furniture, though, that was Grandma's great-great-grandma's, and she won't part with it, no matter how much veneer falls off it or how wobbly it gets."

"Well, I don't blame her," Ann said, walking over to look at an old portrait in an oval frame. "Surely this isn't a reproduction."

"No, no. That's Great-Great-Grandpa Hayden. I almost named my son Hayden, but I wanted him to have his mother's last name, Jessup, and one family name seemed enough for one tiny baby, so in the end I settled on Donovan."

"It's a good name, Donovan Jessup Pryor. But I like Hayden, too. Maybe you can use it for your next child."

Dean looked positively stricken for a moment. Then he lifted a hand, indicating a door at the end of the room near the stove. "Um, this way."

They walked over a rag rug atop a gleaming hardwood floor. Ann noted delicate crocheted doilies and enameled chinaware atop colonial-style tables. Somehow, the flat-screen TV atop the buffet-cum-entertainment center in front of the humpbacked sofa managed to look intrinsic and cozy in the old-fashioned room.

As they entered the dining room, Dean pointed to a chair placed against the wall and said, "Don't sit there. It's not safe. In fact, only the chairs around the table are sturdy enough to sit in."

Because there were five chairs around the table, Ann saw no problem. The size of the sideboard and china cabinet told her that the ornate, rectangular table was missing two, perhaps three, leafs. Ann went straight to the china cabinet, where Betty was setting out plates.

"What a magnificent piece of furniture."

"It's English," Betty told her proudly. "Been in my family seven generations, eight now with

Donovan. Great-Great-Grandpa Dilman Hayden bought it used for Great-Great-Grandma Rosalie at an estate sale in Boston. She gave it to her daughter, Mary Nell, who gave it to her daughter, Susanna, who gave it to her son, Arnold, who passed it down to me. Dean's mother cares nothing for it, but his aunt Deana and I agree that it ought to go to him and then, hopefully, to Donovan or another of Dean's children."

"Grandma," Dean grumbled, "Ann's not interested in our antiques or our family history."

"But I am," Ann refuted brightly. "I think it's beautiful furniture, and I love the history of it. I think you should have it completely restored."

"And how do you suggest we pay for that?" Dean snapped, his hand going to the back of his neck. "The last estimate we got was over a thousand dollars, so we'll just have to make do. Or eat in the kitchen." Betty sent him a troubled look.

Too late, Ann realized that Dean might fear she would find his home and its contents below her standards.

"We eat in the kitchen all the time," she said with a shrug, setting aside her tea to carry the stacked plates to the table, "but if we had this table, I'd insist that we eat in the dining room, even if we had to sit on benches."

Glimpsing the triumphant smile that Betty

shot Dean, Ann walked around the table, setting the plates, which were painted with delicate
pink peonies and drooping bluebells, onto blue
place mats. Dean brought around blue cut-glass
tumblers and grass-green napkins rolled neatly
inside brass rings adorned with pink china peonies.

"It looks like a garden," Ann said, stepping
back.

"Grandma likes her 'pretties,' as she calls
them," Dean commented, placing a set of brass
salt-and-pepper shakers in the center of the table.

"I can see that," Ann told him, walking over
to finger a ruffled doily beneath an impressive
soup tureen on the sideboard. "My mother would
have loved this place. I can almost see her here."

"Oh?"

Ann nodded and put her back to the sideboard.
"I didn't get her domestic gene, I'm afraid, but
I love the history of these things and the conti-
nuity of them."

"Aunt Deana likes modern stuff," Dean said,
trailing a finger along the edge of the table, "but
I don't mind the old stuff, so long as it's serviceable."

"If you take care of things, then they remain
serviceable," she pointed out.

"I do my best," Dean said shortly.

"I know you do."

Donovan came into the room with a basket full of hot biscuits. "Daddy, can I have a biscuit with butter? Please? It won't ruin my dinner, I promise. Grandma says for you to come get the roast."

"I'll get the roast," Dean said, looking askance at his son, "and the butter. Ann, would you see to it that he gets into his booster seat?"

"Happy to."

Donovan didn't need help. He was sitting in his booster seat with an open biscuit on his plate before she could get the chair out from under the table. She shoved it back again while he picked around the edges of the steaming bread. Dean brought in the butter dish and the pot roast then went out again to help Betty carry in the vegetables and tea. Ann buttered Donovan's biscuit and watched him quickly devour the thing, smacking his lips and closing his eyes in ecstasy. Ann had to laugh.

"He loves Grandma's biscuits even more than Callie's cookies," Dean said, placing a pitcher of tea and a bowl of ice cubes on the sideboard.

"Mmm-hmm," Donovan agreed, licking butter from his fingers.

"I don't think I've ever enjoyed anything that much," Ann said.

"Wait until she brings in the honey to go with the biscuits," Dean said, leaning close to speak softly into Ann's ear. Donovan caught the salient word, however, and crowed with delight.

"Honey!"

"*After* you eat your vegetables," Dean dictated.

Donovan wiggled excitedly in his chair and picked up his fork. Shaking his head, Dean walked around and pulled out a chair for Ann then did the same for his grandmother, who entered the room just then with a platter of vegetables to go with the pot roast. He took his own seat at the head of the table. Ann felt sure that he'd been occupying that chair since his grandfather had died. Dean had been all of, what, fifteen years of age then? As he clasped his hands together and bowed his head to pray over the meal, Ann recalled what her father had said about him.

A man fully grown. That was how her father had described Dean, and as usual Wes was correct. Dean had been the owner of this property since the age of fifteen, and when he'd wound up a father at the age of twenty, he'd taken responsibility for his actions, listened to wise counsel, found a solution to his problems and gone to work, surrendering himself to Christ in the process. She, on the other hand, had been a Christian almost her entire life, the product of a loving, two-parent home, raised with every advantage, and she'd let petty insecurities drive her away from her home and the people who loved her most. She felt so foolish.

There was grown, and there was mature. In some ways, Dean was much older than she was. It was time for her to actually grow up.

Chapter Thirteen

"Come up! Come up! Come up and see my room," Donovan urged. "I got the whole attic to myself. Don't I, Dad?"

"You do," Dean confirmed, "but you know the rules. What do we do after meals?"

"Clear the table," Donovan announced. "I ge the salt and pepper. And the butter."

"Just keep your fingers out of the butter," Dean ordered with a chuckle, pushing the dis to the edge of the table so Donovan could reac it. "Then you can take the napkins to the laun dry and put away the napkin rings."

Donovan ran off with the butter dish, whil Dean began gathering plates and Betty starte carrying leftovers to the kitchen. Ann didn't as what she could do, just began picking up glasse and cradling them in the crook of one arm.

"You're going to get your shirt wet doing that," Dean complained. "We'll take care of this."

"It'll dry," she rebutted easily. "I want to help."

Dean frowned, but he said nothing else, just led the way into the kitchen. The large, bright room surprised Ann. By far the most modern room in the house that she'd seen thus far, it boasted tall cabinets painted a soft yellow, mellow gold walls, brick flooring, a metal-topped island, a sweet little maple table and chairs, and white enamel stove unlike anything Ann had ever seen. It had at least three ovens and a grill and five burners. She left the glasses on the metal countertop and went straight to it.

"I have never seen such a cookstove. Mom had something similar but not so big."

Betty grinned broadly. "Amazing, isn't it? Built new in 1940. Milburn bought it used to restore, but he didn't get it finished before he died. We didn't have money for Christmas the year after he passed, but Dean managed to get this back in working order and all shined up like new for me. They don't make them like this anymore." She ran a hand lovingly over the gleaming enamel.

"Mom said the same thing," Ann told her, smiling at Dean.

"A new stove like this costs thousands and thousands of dollars," Betty said proudly.

"It's just an old stove," Dean said, shaking his head.

"It's a work of art!" Ann exclaimed. "Believe me, I've seen hotel kitchens with less."

He shook his head again, but the beginnings of a smile tugged at the corners of his lips. "I believe you're expected upstairs," he said, waving her toward a door that opened into a hallway.

"I am." She smiled at Betty. "I understand that Donovan has the attic all to himself."

The older woman chuckled. "He was promised his dad's old room when he started school. We made the move last week."

"Milestone after milestone," Ann said.

"And coming on fast," Dean grumbled, leading the way.

They passed a bedroom and a bathroom before they came to the narrow stairs. Two more rooms seemed to lay beyond, but he didn't lead her that far down the hall. Instead, they climbed the stairs. Donovan waited halfway up.

"This way! This way!" he called, as if another path might magically appear.

There was no door. The staircase, surrounded by tall railings, opened right into the middle of the long, narrow space. A desk had been placed beneath a window at the end of the room. Donovan's backpack rested atop it. A narrow bed had been tucked into the corner on one side of he railing, along with a dresser and chair. The other side of the room was basically one long wall of shelves and cubbyholes with a space at the end for a closet.

Donovan twirled in the space before the desk, his arms outstretched, and cried, "Ta-da!"

"Utterly perfect," Ann pronounced, taking it all in. She looked at Dean, who remained on the stairs, his arms braced on the railings. "This was your room?"

"Until I went to college," he confirmed. "After Donovan was born, it was easier to be downstairs with him in the room next to me."

"I'm gonna live here forever!" Donovan exclaimed.

Ann laughed. "It is a fun room."

She let the boy show her all of his most treasured possessions, including the photo album that he kept under his bed. He had photos of the mother and great-grandfather he'd never met, as well as his grandmother, Dean's mother, whom he called by her given name, Wynona. Obviously Wynona had taken after her father, Milburn in looks, and so had Dean. Sadly, she didn't seem to have inherited either of her parents' sense of responsibility. Thankfully, Dean had.

"Wynona comes around sometimes," Donovan said offhandedly, closing the album with a snap. "Mostly it just makes Grandma mad when she does, though. I wish you could come on Wednesday," he whined. "You know, just for the first time."

"Well," Ann said, wrapping her arms around him as they sat there on the edge of his bed, "it just so happens that I don't have to go to the city until Wednesday afternoon."

Catching his breath, Donovan tilted his head back and looked up at her. She winked, and he whooped.

"Yippee!" Twisting, he threw an arm around her neck, toppling her onto the bed. Suddenly he scrambled up. "Hey, now I got a dad *and a* mom to take me. Well, sort of a mom."

Ann willed back a sudden rush of tears, smiled and said, "A substitute mom. A—a stand-in."

"Yeah." He beamed. "A sustitude mom. I gotta tell Grandma!"

He tore around the end of the railing. Dean stepped up out of his way, admonishing Donovan to slow down. Ann rose from the bed to follow in the boy's happy wake, but she didn't make it past his father. Dean lifted his hands to her shoulders, where they hovered uncertainly.

"You didn't have to do that," he said softly.

"But I wanted to."

Sighing, he finally brought his hands to gently frame her face. She closed her eyes, feeling the sweetly magnetic pull that had only ever existed with this man, and willed him to kiss her. In the end, however, he kissed not her lips but her forehead. She tried not to be disappointed, tried not to fear that he had thought better of an involvement with her now that he knew she was actually available. As she walked down those stairs, however, she knew that while she might be a very welcome substitute mom to Donovan, she had absolutely no reason to hope that she might one day be a beloved wife to his father.

Substitute mother did not equal wife. Dean reminded himself of that fact over and over again throughout the coming days and nights. He kept as busy as he could, which wasn't difficult, given that he'd arranged to take off the rest of the week after school started, so he had lots to do before then. Both he and Donovan had some serious adjustments to make, and he wanted to be readily available if the school called to say that Donovan was having a difficult time. At least that was what he told himself. The truth was that he was dreading going back out into the field without his son at his side.

He remembered what it had been like when Donovan was a baby. No one could be better suited to caring for an infant than Grandma Betty, but Dean had felt an irrational fear and resentment at having to be away from his son all day. He'd made a point of returning to the house for lunch just to hold and cuddle the miraculous little bundle of humanity that had so radically changed his life. As soon as Donovan was out of diapers—and that was earlier than with many children—Dean had started taking the boy with him.

Those days were over now, and Dean felt as if his whole life had upended yet again. It was foolish to feel such emptiness just because Donovan was starting school. If he couldn't handle this, what would happen to him when Donovan actually left home?

He and Ann hadn't discussed arrangements for Donovan's first day of school. Dean had avoided doing so because he didn't want her to know what a difficult time he had talking about it. Grandma had decided that she would be better off staying home; she didn't want to cry in front of Donovan for fear he would conclude that school was a bad thing. Dean was feeling pretty emotional about it himself, though he could feign enthusiasm without tears. As for Donovan, he bubbled with excitement and at the same time felt obvious trepidation. Dean didn't know which one of them was more pleased when they walked out the front door of the house on Wednesday morning and found Ann waiting for them.

Dressed in jeans, boots and a pretty blouse

her long, straight hair hanging from a simple side part, she leaned against the fender of a white metallic BMW two-door coupe with a deep red interior.

"I hope you don't mind," she said. "I switched Donovan's safety seat from your backseat to mine."

That sleek, low, expensive automobile demonstrated the chasm between them as little else could, but Dean couldn't find it in him to protest. Ann was a successful woman. She deserved a fine car, and what could it hurt?

He lifted an eyebrow at his son. "Riding in style."

Whooping, Donovan ran for the Beemer. Dean followed more circumspectly, watching Ann help Donovan belt himself into the seat. To his surprise, as soon as he drew near, she tossed him the key fob then got into the car on the passenger side. He didn't argue, just walked around, removed his hat and dropped down behind the steering wheel.

"It's been a while since I drove a car," he admitted.

She chuckled. "Somehow I think you can manage."

He needed a little while to figure out how to start the thing. It had no key. He soon had them on the road, however. Donovan was fascinated by the video display. Used to the dually pickup truck, Dean found the interior somewhat tight, but he loved the way the vehicle handled. When they pulled into the school parking lot, Dean realized with a shock that he hadn't fretted a bit on the trip into town. He'd been too much focused on the experience of driving Ann's sweet little ride to even think about their destination. Giving her a direct look as he slapped the key fob into her palm, he silently wondered if she'd planned that.

She smiled and said, "I was enthralled for a full month after I first bought this thing."

Dean shook his head, but he was smiling, too. "You're scary, you know that?"

"I didn't think a clever woman would frighten you," she quipped, opening her door.

They all got out and headed into the building, Donovan bouncing excitedly between Dean and Ann. Fifteen or twenty other kindergarteners beat along the same path. About half seemed to be accompanied by two parents. Some were younger children ushered in by older siblings and mothers. A few had parents and some grandparents along. Clearly, Donovan would have been the only child escorted by his father only.

Donovan's teacher knew both Dean and Ann. She also clearly knew that they weren't married, but she diplomatically avoided addressing either of them in any way that called attention to that fact. If she was surprised to see them together, she hid it well.

While Dean signed a permission slip to allow Donovan to have chocolate milk that morning, Ann helped Donovan find his assigned cubby and hang up his backpack. The teacher said they would unpack their supplies later. Then it was time for hugs and goodbyes. Suddenly, Donovan turned up shy, clinging to both Dean and Ann. For the first time Dean felt tongue-tied when it came to his son. He simply did not know what to say at that moment. Ann, however, did.

She knelt and smoothed the collar of Donovan's striped knit shirt, softly saying, "Do you know, I think you're the biggest boy in the room. When I was a girl in school, I had a friend who was the biggest boy in the room. He was also the nicest boy, always smiling and sharing. He made me feel so safe. Your class is blessed to have you because you're the nicest boy I know."

Donovan beamed. The teacher astutely pointed him to an activity, asking if he knew how it worked. When he replied that he did, she suggested that he help others with it. He proudly ran off to do that. A friend from church joined him at the table, and just like that he was laughing and happy. Suddenly, Dean realized, his son was a schoolkid.

A space seemed to open inside Dean's chest. He gulped, feeling a lump in his throat and the unexpected blur of tears. Without a word he strode out into the hallway and headed for the parking lot. Ann caught up to him just as he pushed through the door. The instant it clanged shut behind him, she grabbed his hand, yanking him to a halt. Then she was on her tiptoes in front of him, her arms about his neck in a ferocious hug. He couldn't do anything except put his head on her shoulder and hug her back.

"Ridiculous," he muttered apologetically.

She shook her head. "No," she whispered. "It's wonderful." Somehow that was all he needed to regain control. Sighing, he straightened. She took him by the hand and towed him toward the car, saying, "Let's get some coffee."

That sounded very good. Dean felt strangely deflated and exhausted.

Ann drove them over to the diner. There they chose a table in the corner and settled in to nurse cups of coffee so strong that Dean almost couldn't drink it. He got enough of it down to temper the rest of it with cream. Then the waitress topped off the cup, and he was right back where he'd started. He thought a piece of pie might make the brew more palatable, and he was right, so he ate another, and all the while, Ann held his hand and he talked.

"I know it's stupid to be this broken up about my kid starting school," he admitted. "It's just that I'm so used to having him around, you know?"

"He knocks out every step you make all day, every day."

"Some folks think having him out there isn't safe, but I figure with me is the safest place he can be. I always know where he is and what he's doing."

"I realize that."

"He never gets into trouble, and he's learned a lot just being around while I work, you know?"

"No doubt about it."

"You hear about bad things happening in schools," he worried aloud.

"In War Bonnet?"

He shoved a hand through his hair. "Of course not. I'm being stupid."

"You're being a great father," she countered.

"I offered to marry his mother," Dean divulged quietly, needing Ann to know that. "She wanted no part of me. Or him. She'd have aborted or given him up for adoption if I hadn't insisted on taking custody."

"Were you in love with her?" Ann asked.

"Not at all. I met her at a party one night."

"You were young. You made a mistake," Ann

said, clasping his hand, "but then you stepped up and did all the right things after."

"So far all I've had to do is love him, feed him, house him, clothe him and keep him clean." Dean chuckled. "The last has been the hardest part." His amusement dwindled. "Honestly, feeding, housing and clothing him hasn't exactly been a piece of cake."

"That was the whole point of the business plan," Ann said.

Realizing that the time had come to address that issue forthrightly, Dean sat back in his chair, pulling his hand from hers.

"Jolly, I appreciate your work on that, but I've got to tell you. That plan of yours is just so much pie in the sky." She cocked her head, staring at him solemnly. He sat forward again, folding his arms along the edge of the tabletop. "Sweetheart, I'll never have the kind of capital your plan calls for. I wouldn't borrow it even if I could, which I cannot. And I won't sell my grandmother's home out from under her. Not only did she raise me as her own, she's helping to raise my son. And you may not know this, but when my grandpa died, he left everything to me. Not to Grandma. To *me*. He trusted me to take care of her, and I'll do that to her last breath. Or mine. It's a great business plan, and I'd love to put it into effect but I don't see any way to make it happen. Those are just the facts. I'm sorry to disappoint you."

Ann smiled, softly, warmly. "I don't think you could disappoint me if you tried."

He took her hand again, squeezing it gently. "Thank you for that."

"What about an investor?"

Blinking at her, he needed a moment to process that idea. "An investor? Who would invest in me? Please tell me you didn't ask your dad—"

"No, no. Not with him so ill."

Dean relaxed somewhat. "Good. He's done enough for me already."

"He's quite a fan of yours," Ann said, "but this is someone who wants to invest in War Bonnet."

"Oh?"

"Someone who's been away for a while and... misses it."

"But what does that have to do with me?"

She took a deep breath, not quite meeting his gaze any longer. "Well, it's someone who's looking for something to *do* around here." She paused then softly added, "Someone who doesn't want to go back where she came from."

Dean's heart *thunked* inside his chest and then began to speed up. He flattened his hands against the tabletop.

"Where *she* came from?" he repeated. Ann nodded without looking at him. Dean could hardly speak, his heart was racing so fast. "And did *she* come from Dallas?"

Ann looked at him then, saying urgently. "I have the money, Dean."

"You have the money," he said, trying to wrap his mind around this. "Where? In, like, a retirement fund or something?"

"No! I wouldn't touch that," Ann assured him. Dean knew that he was gaping at her, but he couldn't seem to help himself. "I have savings, investments. I've been making six figures for five years, Dean, and I don't even pay rent."

"And you want to move back to War Bonnet," he asked, thumping the tabletop with a finger for emphasis, "to invest in a custom farming business? Farming without an actual farm. Farming for other people."

She looked him straight in the eye then, and the smile she gave him both melted his insides and sent his hopes soaring.

"Sort of," she said huskily. "What I really want to invest in is *you*. I believe in you, Dean, in who and what you are."

Dumbfounded, Dean sat back in his chair, rubbed a hand over his face and silently asked God how this could possibly work.

Could he take her money, work alongside her day after day, grow his business, raise his standard of living and have a chance to make her more than a business partner? He had no doubt that she knew her stuff, that she could help him, but was it more than that? Could it be more than that?

Her heart in her throat, Ann waited for Dean's response to her proposal, but he simply stared at her.

Just then the phone behind the cash register jangled. Ann's nerve endings jangled, as well, and she glanced in that direction. Jenny, the middle-aged waitress, appeared and plucked up the receiver.

"Diner." She listened for a few moments, made a face and glanced around, her gaze alighting on Dean and Ann. "I'll see what I can do." Lowering the receiver, she called across the room. "Hey, Dean, think you could do me a favor?"

Dean twisted around on his chair. "Sure, Jenny. What's up?"

"Your bill's on the house if you can run an order over to the high school for me."

Dean looked at Ann, who shrugged. "I've got nothing going until we pick up Donovan from school at noon."

Turning back to the waitress and rising from his chair, Dean said, "We'll take that deal, Jenny."

Shooting him a thumbs-up signal, Jenny spoke

into the phone. "It'll be right over." She hung up and smiled at Dean. "One second. It's waiting in the kitchen."

While Ann gathered her small handbag, dropped a tip on the table and rose, Dean strolled over to the counter. Ann arrived at almost the same moment as Jenny and the cook did. The pair of them bore a large brown paper bag stuffed to the max and a flat, rectangular cardboard box.

"This needs to go to Coach Lyons's office. They got some kind of meeting going on and some confusion about whoever was supposed to pick up the food. The school runs a tab and pays for it monthly, so you won't have to worry about collecting money."

"Okay."

"You'll want to go to the field house behind the ball field and—"

"I know where it is," Dean interrupted.

"Don't set anything on top of this box," Jenny instructed, placing the box on the countertop. "It's filled with those lemon crème pastries Coach loves."

"He's still eating those things?"

"Every chance he gets." She leaned close and muttered out of the corner of her mouth, "We buy 'em frozen and nuke 'em in the microwave, but don't tell him that."

Dean chuckled. "Your secret's safe with me."

Ann smiled, remembering with bittersweet poignancy the lemon crème pastries that she had delivered to Coach's office in the past. All the kids had known that they were his special weakness and had often plied him with lemon crèmes when begging forgiveness for some failure or misdeed. Ann had sprung for half a dozen during her sophomore year after blowing off several hours of softball camp at Oklahoma State University to run around Stillwater with her friends. They'd felt so sophisticated, hitting all the most popular college hangouts, where they went virtually unnoticed, only to return to find that they'd missed out on a meet-and-greet with the women's softball team, men's baseball team and the university athletic recruiters. Coach's disappointment had been palpable.

"Do you want a scholarship or not, Billings?" he'd demanded.

She'd privately vowed never to disappoint him again and had sincerely concentrated on her game after that. Before long he'd started giving her the extra batting practice, and then had come the nickname Jolly. She'd gotten her scholarship, and she'd thought she'd earned Coach's regard. But then she'd learned what Coach *really* thought of her, and the truth had upended her world.

Jenny patted Dean's cheek. He slid the box toward Ann and took the much heavier sack from the cook. As she turned toward the door, the thought occurred to Ann that the moment had come to face the darkest, most foolish part of her past. How could she ever truly come home if she didn't somehow put that crushing moment to rest? As Ann drove toward the ballpark where she had spent so many hours, she wondered just how best to do that.

Should she speak to Coach, ask him about that day? From time to time she'd thought about doing just that, but what if he didn't even remember saying those things about her? What if he denied saying them?

Part of her wanted to go to her dad as she no doubt should have done in the very beginning, but the circumstances of his illness argued against that, certainly in the short-term. She could wait until he felt better, of course. He was violently ill immediately after every treatment, but then he gradually got better—better being a relative word as each treatment seemed to take more out of him than the last. Eventually the cancer would be defeated, and his body would begin to recover from the treatment. At least that was the hope.

Her gaze wandered to Dean, but the last man with whom she had shared that life-altering event had used it to pull the wool over her eyes. She had shown him her weakness, and he had used it against her. What else explained that engagement scheme? She had difficulty believing that Dean compared in any way to Jordan, but how could she trust her own judgment at this point?

Maybe if they were business partners, if Dean decided to let her invest in his business, maybe that would change everything. Maybe they would develop the kind of trust and honesty that would allow her to confide in him.

Oh, who was she kidding?

She wasn't looking for a business opportunity. She just wanted a chance for Dean to fall in love with her. The way she had fallen in love with him.

Even before she'd discovered the horrid truth about Jordan, she'd fallen in love with Dean. If she was perfectly honest with herself, she'd felt a secret sense of relief because Jordan had given her a valid excuse to break their engagement. Yes, she'd been crushed to learn that he didn't value her at all except as a means to an end. Personally she meant nothing to Jordan. She realized now, though, that she hadn't really valued Jordan as she should have, either.

His main value to her had rested simply in the supposed fact that he loved her. She hadn't loved

Jordan for Jordan; she'd loved the idea that Jordan loved her. When that proved not to be true, her fragile ego had taken a definite beating, but in some ways she'd been relieved.

It stunned Ann to know that, had it been Dean whose career could be boosted through marriage to her, she'd have gone through with it simply for his sake, even knowing that he didn't love her as she loved him. The undeniable truth was that she wanted what was best for Dean and Donovan, even if it wasn't what was best for her.

So if a business partnership was all she could have with Dean, then she'd settle for that and work to make that business boom and their lives better. But she'd pray for more.

She would pray unceasingly for more.

Chapter Fourteen

"Déjà vu all over again," Dean quipped as Ann drove around the heavy chain-link fence wrapping the spotty field. "They never could get the grass to grow properly."

"Hey, it's Oklahoma, land of three seasons," she shot back.

They said it together. "Freezing, blistering and tornado."

"With emphasis on the blistering," Dean said as she parked the car behind the long, squat building that housed the locker and weight rooms along with the coaches' offices.

Ann opened her door and got out. "Actually, it's hotter in Texas." She shook her head. "Not colder, though."

Dean followed suit, pointing out, tongue in cheek, "And we haven't had a real tornado in decades."

"There is that," she agreed, straight-faced. "Not to mention the two weeks of spring and autumn we enjoy every year."

Dean chuckled, wondering just why it was that she really wanted to come home. Did her job disappear along with her engagement? Or did she really want to be here?

"There's better weather," he said drily, "but what other place on earth has red-orange dirt?"

"So true," she agreed, playing along.

They both laughed as they gathered their packages and trudged across the graveled parking area to the entrance. Dean pulled open the metal door and stood back to let Ann enter first. The telescoping room divider that blocked off the workout room when it was in use had been pushed back, revealing an empty space. The weight benches, treadmills and other machines all stood abandoned and quiet. The showers, which opened off the workout room, were dark and silent. Both boys and girls used the facility but at different times.

Peg Amber, the girls' basketball coach, stepped out into a hallway on the right. A bright smile split her face, showing overlarge teeth and healthy pink gums.

"Dean! What are you doing here?"

"Delivering food. Coach Amber, do you know Ann Billings?"

The other woman came forward. Dressed in baggy workout clothes, her brown hair caught in a short ponytail at the back of her head, she stood almost as tall as Dean, every inch the female jock. "Don't think so." Her eyes suddenly lit as she took in Ann. "Billings," she repeated. "You wouldn't be Jolly Billings?"

Ann smiled limply. "The same."

Amber waved a hand, grinning. "You were before my day, but Lyons never stops bragging about you."

"Oh?"

"Baseball and softball are where his heart is, you know," Coach Amber said. "Most athletic directors are all football all the time with basketball coming in a distant second and everything else kind of hanging on by sheer determination. But Lyons is all about the diamond. Makes him more fair with the other sports, I think. As far as softball goes, though, there'll never be another Jolly Billings."

Ann blinked at that, though Dean couldn't imagine why she would be surprised. "I, uh, think we're supposed to leave this food in Coach Lyons's office," he quickly said.

"Actually it's the conference room next door," Peg Amber corrected, signaling them to follow her. Glancing at the box Ann carried, she asked, "Would those be lemon crèmes?"

"They would."

"Yum."

Dean traded an amused glance with Ann and followed Coach Amber down the hallway. She stopped and stuck her head into one room, calling, "Jack! Food's here."

Jack Lyons popped out into the hallway, pulling dollar bills out of his pocket. He froze when he saw Dean and Ann.

"Coach," Dean greeted the older man.

"Well, I'll be! What're you two doing here? Didn't expect a couple of my old favorites to turn up on the first day of school, delivering for the diner, of all things."

"How's it going?" Dean asked.

"Hectic as usual," came the reply. He stuffed the bills back into his pocket, took the bag from Dean and passed it to Peg, saying, "Y'all get started. I'll be there in a minute."

Nodding, she carried the bag into the next room. Ann handed the box of pastries to Lyons. "Mmm-mmm," he hummed. Winking at Dean, he said, "Not the first time this has happened, is it, Jolly?"

"No, sir," she said, smiling down at her feet.

"Now tell me. How'd the two of you wind up delivering food for the diner?"

"Well, I dropped my boy off at his first day of kindergarten this morning," Dean began.

"Is he a big boy like you?"

"He is."

"Is he going to play ball?"

Dean chuckled. "I imagine so. We'll see."

"I'll be on the lookout for him."

"Don't rush him." Dean chuckled. "I'm having enough trouble with the idea of him starting school. Ann had to take me down to the diner for a cup of consolation coffee, which is how we happened to be there when Jenny needed help."

Lyons grinned. "Oh, you single parents. They all grow up. Just look at you." He turned his attention to Ann then, asking, "How's your dad?"

"In Oklahoma City getting treatment. Should be home this evening."

"Sure hope he beats this thing," Coach said seriously.

"We're counting on it," Ann told him, "and praying that way."

Lyons nodded. "Guess you'll be heading back to Dallas soon. I saw Rex in town yesterday."

"Actually," Ann said, parking her hands at her waist, "I don't think I'll be going back, after all."

He gaped at her then looked pointedly to her hand. "So the wedding is off?"

"It's off," she confirmed, looking at Dean. "Seems that what I want is here in War Bonnet. And what he wants is someplace else."

"Well, I'll be," Lyons declared. Then he smiled

broadly. "You know what they say. There's no place like home."

Ann smiled wanly. "That is so true."

"So what are you going to do?" Coach Lyons asked. "Jobs don't exactly grow on trees around here, you know."

"I'll find something," Ann said, glancing at Dean. "Sometimes you have to make your own job, like Dean did."

"That is a true statement," Lyons said, clapping Dean on the shoulder with one hand. "He sure did do that." Lyons shook a finger at her, adding, "And if anybody else can do it, Jolly girl, you can. You were always best and brightest."

"Thank you."

"Well, I better get in there," he said, backing away. "Don't y'all be strangers now. Come on by and visit when you can."

"Sure thing," Dean said.

Coach Lyons went into the conference room, carrying his box of pastries, and closed the door behind him.

Sighing, Ann put her back to the wall and bowed her head. After a moment she said, "That's the man who drove me out of War Bonnet."

Astounded, Dean gaped at her. *"What?"*

"It happened right here," she said quietly. "In this very spot."

Dean seized her by the upper arms, appalled and suddenly frightened. What had Coach done?

"Honey, what are you talking about?" he demanded softly.

She leaned into him, tucking her head beneath his chin and laying her face against his chest. "Dean, I'm such a fool," she whispered. "Such an idiotic fool."

More worried than ever and suddenly aware of their surroundings, Dean turned toward the exit at the far end of the hall. He walked her straight out onto the field and down into the dugout where they had spent so much of their youth. There, he gently pushed her down onto the bench, sat beside her and took her hands in his.

"Tell me. All of it. What did Lyons do to you?"

She shook her head. "Oh, it's not fair to blame him," she admitted. "It was much more me than him. He didn't even know he'd done it."

Dean edged around to more fully face her. "What are you saying?"

She waved an arm at their surroundings. "You remember how I was back then, Dean. All about the game. Taking batting practice with the boys."

"And outslugging half of them," Dean said matter-of-factly. Ann grimaced. "What? It's true," he insisted. "You're deadly with a bat."

"Mmm-hmm, as deadly as any man."

"I wouldn't go that far," he muttered, "but you could hold your own back then. That's something to be proud of."

"Is it? I thought so. Then one day I came home from college to visit, and I naturally swung by here to see Coach Lyons. It was something I did routinely."

"Yeah, I did it a few times, too," Dean commented.

"I did it *a lot*," Ann confessed. "I was so homesick. Even in my junior year at college, I still just wanted to be done with it and get back home. I thought I'd work at the bank and then maybe take over the ranch when Dad was ready to retire. Rex had gone to law school and always said he wanted no part of the ranch, so I thought, why not me?"

"What happened?" Dean asked again, squeezing her hand.

Ann sighed, staring at her lap. "Well, I stopped by as soon as school was out. I always stopped after hours. Anyway, as I walked up to Coach's office, I heard him talking to one of the teachers. About me."

Dean's brow wrinkled. "What about you?"

Ann sighed. "He called me awkward, said I was taller than half the male population, could outslug most of the teenage boys I'd worked out with and that if you cut off my hair you wouldn't be able to tell the difference between me and them."

Dean frowned. *That* was the terrible secret that had driven her away from War Bonnet? He rubbed both hands over his face then abruptly dropped them as he remembered another time she had confided in him, the questions she had asked.

Do you think I'm feminine? What, specifically, is womanly about me?

She'd worried that she was too tall, that her shoulders were too broad, her nose too long and her jaw too square.

Finally it all made sense. The coach she had worked so hard for, the man she'd admired and respected, had disparaged her and destroyed her self-confidence. Given his prominence in this small town, what else was she going to do but run?

"I don't know why Coach would say such a thing," Dean declared, "but it's the most absurd bunk I've ever heard. You were the hottest thing War Bonnet had ever seen! You still are!"

Ann smiled and ran her fingertips down his cheek, sucking in a shaky breath. "Caroline said—"

"Caroline Carmody?" Caroline Carmody had taught English at War Bonnet for a few years back then. She'd been a shapely blonde that all the boys had ogled.

"Yes. Caroline said that I'd probably wind up an old maid living with my parents."

"Ann," Dean said, suddenly sure what had happened, "Lyons was dating Caroline back then."

"What?"

"Everyone knew it. Everyone who was still in school. I was a senior. It was all the talk. She was probably jealous as all get-out."

"Jealous?"

"Think about it. His favorite *former* female student, a gorgeous redhead, dropping by all the time. Lyons was probably trying to soothe Caroline. That's all. He couldn't have meant those things. He's not that blind or stupid." Dean stood, pulling her up with him. "But you were."

"What?"

"Put yourself in his position, sweetheart. You were—are—gorgeous. And by then you were no longer off-limits."

"But he was my coach."

"Not anymore. You were three years out of school, babe. No wonder Caroline was nervous. The problem wasn't that you were unattractive or unfeminine. It was just the opposite."

The incredulous look on her face made Dean want to hug her.

"You think?"

"Jolly, if I'd known you were coming around to see Lyons back then, I'd have been jealous," he confessed, smoothing her hair with his hands.

She grinned. "Really?"

Dean rolled his eyes heavenward, dropping his hands to her shoulders. "Don't you get it yet? I had the world's biggest crush on you!"

Her eyes and her mouth rounded in surprise. "I really was blind and stupid, wasn't I?" she commented, sounding stunned.

A door slammed somewhere and voices could be heard drawing closer to the dugout.

Dean grabbed Ann's hand, leading her across the dugout to the opposite end. "Come on. We're leaving."

"Okay," she agreed without hesitation. "Where are we going?"

"Someplace more private," he muttered, racking his brain for just such a spot.

"In that case," she said, dangling the Beemer's key fob in front of him, "you might need this."

He grabbed the fob with his free hand, but in his heart of hearts he knew that he already had what he needed in his *other* hand. The problem was, given the many differences still between them, he didn't quite know how to keep her.

* * *

I had the world's biggest crush on you. Had.
That one word in an otherwise dreamy sentence
needled Ann.

Well, she wanted more than a crush from him
now. She wanted, oh, everything, absolutely everything. But now that he knew just how idiotic
she had been all these years, could he possibly
feel for her what she wanted, needed, him to
feel? If he'd just agree to the business partnership, she might have a chance to show him that
she'd finally wised up. She knew that she could
be an asset to him when it came to the business
and if it didn't work out the way she wanted in
the end, at least he and Donovan would be better off financially.

Please, God, she prayed as Dean drove them
around, seemingly aimlessly. *I've been so foolish for so long. I know better now. It's not that
I think I'm suddenly some hot number all men
want. If that were true, I'd have gotten over this
nonsense long ago.* But other men had shown
interest in her, she realized, interest she had dis-
couraged for fear they would discover how lacking she was in feminine attributes. *I understand
now that You made me as complete as every
other woman, and I let one carelessly overheard
conversation shake my confidence in myself and
You. That was stupid, and I'm sorry, Lord.*

Finally, Dean brought the car to a stop at the end of a shady lane near an uncharacteristically blue body of water.

"This is Clear Springs Lake."

"Can't think of a cooler spot," he said, killing the engine and rolling down the windows.

The small lake, which was fed by a spring, sat on private property, but the owners had never begrudged the public access to the site, posting numerous signs denying any responsibility for injury or loss. The local kids were known to make good use of the spot, especially at night. As a result, this place had long held a reputation as the local lovers' lane.

"Might be cooler if we get out," Dean said, opening his door.

The rear of the car was better shaded than the front, and the engine compartment was bound to be hot, so they leaned against the trunk, feet crossed at the ankles. Ann braced her hands on the vehicle behind her. Dean folded his arms.

"I can't believe you just accepted what Lyons was saying about you as fact," Dean finally said. "I mean, you have a mirror."

"No woman trusts what she sees in the mirror," Ann muttered.

"There had to be guys buzzing around you. I went to college, you know."

"Not for me," Ann told him softly. "I wasn't

raised like that. Once I let enough guys know that, they stopped *buzzing,* as you put it."

Dean smiled. "Good for you. Wish I'd been that smart. But then I wouldn't have Donovan."

"We all make mistakes," she said. "It's how you handle them that counts. I may not have handled Lyons's criticisms well, but Dean, I know what I'm doing when it comes to business."

He nodded. "I don't doubt it. What about your job, though?"

"I'm going to resign. I don't want to work for LHI anymore."

"There must be other jobs."

"There are, but I want to be here."

"And you truly have the money to invest?"

"I wouldn't lie to you."

He dropped his arms. "Well, that leaves jus one problem, then."

"What's that?"

"I can't take your money. Unless you marr me."

Ann nearly fell down, too stunned to reac with anything but shock. "Dean!"

He shifted, finally looking at her, the heat i his eyes melting her heart. "I've loved you ha my life already," he said softly, "literally half m life. I'll always love you. I can't work with yo and pretend that I—"

She threw herself on him. "Yes! Of course I'll marry you! I'm crazy in love with you!"

He laughed, clamping one arm around her waist and pushing away from the car with the other. "I was beginning to get the idea, but you've been out of reach for so long, I—I couldn't quite convince myself it could be true."

Wrapping herself around him, she kissed him until he swept her into his arms and swung her in a circle, laughing. But then he sobered, setting her on her feet.

"Wait, wait. You need to know something. About Grandma. I promised she'd always have a home with me, and I'll never go against that. Grandpa trusted me to take care of her."

Ann kissed him into silence. "We'd starve without your grandmother in the house. I thought we'd established that I'm not exactly domestic. I mean, I'm willing to learn, but…don't get your hopes up."

Dean chuckled and put his forehead to hers. "So Grandma's safe. And there's always the diner."

"And Callie," Ann added.

"I have to think you're okay with kids because here is Donovan," Dean said.

"Would you like more children?" Ann asked carefully.

"I would," he stated, squaring his shoulders.

"I like being a dad, and it would be nice to do it right."

She smiled. "I think you've done quite well, but it would be fun to do it together. I can't wait to tell Donovan!"

Dean relaxed, glancing at his watch. "Still too early."

"We could tell Rex and Callie."

"Yeah, let's do that," Dean agreed, grinning. "I feel like I'm going to bust if I don't tell someone."

"My dad's going to be so happy," Ann proclaimed. "He likes you so much."

"There's no one I respect more than your dad," Dean told her. "Oh, man, I can't believe this. Who would've thought that after all this time…" He cupped her face in his hands. "It's proof positive that God does answer prayer."

She went up on tiptoe, wrapped her arms around his neck and kissed him with all the love in her heart. Answered prayers, indeed.

Chapter Fifteen

❧

"What do you think?" Ann asked, showing Callie the gold satin suit. "It's not white, but I haven't worn it, and it's very expensive. Plus, I have shoes to match."

She'd brought the suit thinking that Jordan might drive down one weekend, and she'd wanted something stunning to wear to church while he was here, something that would tell everyone in War Bonnet how well she'd done, just in case Jordan hadn't impressed everyone enough. Silly, silly girl. She was so happy that she no longer thought like that. She'd never feel the need to impress anyone again. What a blessing!

"It's gorgeous," Callie told her, "and I've got something I think will make it just right for a wedding."

She hurried from the bedroom, leaving Ann

to find the shoes that matched the suit. Rex was out on the range, so they'd left Dean downstairs with baby Bodie. He was an old hand with little ones, after all. Callie returned within moments, carrying a small, flat, round box. From it she drew a headband of white silk flowers with pearl centers and a face veil of wide netting that ended just below the nose. "I bought this for my own wedding, but then I found something that worked better with my dress. I meant to return it, but I'd be happy to give it to you if you think it works."

Ann tried it on, holding up the suit in front of the mirror. With her hair combed back and hanging straight, the sophisticated little veil worked very well. "I like it. Simple white bouquet, pearl earrings and I'm set."

"It's lovely," Callie agreed, hugging her. "I'm so happy for you. I think I heard Rex's truck pulling up when I was in the other room. He'll be surprised, but he really likes Dean, you know. Everyone does."

"He's so wonderful, Callie," Ann said softly.

"The man you love is always wonderful."

The two women laughed, and Ann sighed happily.

Just then, Dean called up the stairs. "Ann? Honey? Your brother's here."

"Coming!"

She laid aside the suit and the veil and hurried down the stairs, Callie on her heels. The men were standing in the foyer, staring at each other. Dean had Bodie tucked into the curve of his arm. Rex plopped his sweat-stained straw cowboy hat onto a peg on the wall and looked up the stairs, his pale blue gaze targeting Ann.

"Honey?" he echoed, eyebrows raised.

Dean cleared his throat, sending Ann a sheepish, apologetic glance. At the same time, Callie snorted behind Ann.

"Yes, well, there are things you don't know," Ann said primly, suppressing her smile as he descended the remaining stairs.

"For instance?" Rex asked, hanging an elbow on the banister at the foot of those stairs.

"For instance," Ann said, slipping past him to stand at Dean's side, "we're getting married."

Rex turned his head to glance at his wife then looked once more to Ann. "You and Dean are getting married?"

Ann grinned and threaded her arm through Dean's. "That's right. The sooner, the better."

Rex tilted his dark head. "Because?"

"Because we love each other, of course." Ann said, frowning.

"And that's the only reason?" Rex prodded.

"The *only* reason," Dean answered in a steely

voice that had Bodie grabbing his shirt and crawling onto his chest.

Callie quietly came down the stairs and took her daughter in hand, shooting Ann a supportive look. "Let's sit down and discuss this like adults, everyone."

"What's to discuss?" Ann wanted to know, even as Rex followed Callie and the baby into the living room and Dean pressed his hand into the small of her back, urging her to go along.

"What's to discuss," Rex said, dropping into their father's chair, "is someone named Jordan Teel."

Ann made a show of sitting calmly on the sofa and crossing her legs. Dean came down beside her, stretching his long arm out behind her shoulders. Callie chose the rocker, nine-month-old Bodie in her lap.

"I broke it off with Jordan some time ago," Ann announced. "You weren't here so you wouldn't know." Actually no one had known except Dean and then her father.

"And you broke it off with Jordan because?"

"Don't see how that's any of your business really," Dean said lightly, and Ann fell in love with him all over again. Clearly he was trying to spare her the humiliation of revealing Jordan's treachery. She smiled and patted Dean's knee.

"He was using me to advance his career," she

said bluntly. "I don't suppose I'd have minded if I'd been in love with him, but I wasn't."

Rex inclined his head in acceptance. "What about *your* career?"

"I think I'm done with hotel management. Have been for some time, really. I have other business interests now."

Her brother seemed to consider this for several moments. "That aside, have you two thought about where you'll live?"

"That's all settled," Dean said. "I do have a house."

"So you're staying in War Bonnet?" Rex asked Ann. "You really think you'll be happy here?"

"I'm sure of it."

"I don't know, sis," Rex said doubtfully, shaking his head. "Moving from the city to the country is a big adjustment. Take it from me. And what about that spectacular Dallas wedding you had your heart set on?"

"I don't want or need that anymore." She looked to Dean then, adding, "I haven't got anything to prove to anybody now." She shifted closer to him, saying to her brother, "I just want Dean and Donovan. That's all I need."

"You've only known him a few weeks," Rex pointed out.

"I've known him since he was thirteen!" Ann refuted, conveniently omitting the fact that she'd barely registered his existence for most of those years.

"Oh, yeah? What size shoe does he wear? What size ring?"

Ann felt heat stain her cheeks.

"Size twelve shoe. Size thirteen ring," Dean replied calmly. "Callie know that stuff about you when she agreed to marry you?"

Over in the rocking chair, Callie bent her head to hide a smile. Ann ignored all of it, taking Dean's hand in both of hers.

"He's got hands like Dad," she said defiantly, "the hands of an honest, capable, hardworking man. I think I started falling in love with him the day I first saw his hands."

Dean curled his fingers through hers, smiling down at her.

"Annie, since you brought up Donovan, it has to be said," Rex went on doggedly, "your whole life I've never heard you talk about wanting to be a mother."

Truth time. Ann sucked in a deep breath. "I honestly didn't know if I wanted children," she admitted, "until Donovan. But how can you not love that kid? And Dean is such a wonderful father. Watching the two of them is amazing. Who wouldn't want more of that?"

Dean dropped his arm from the back of the sofa and drew it tightly about her, vowing,

"We're getting married, and that's all there is to it."

"Well, at least give it some time," Rex pleaded. "You don't have to run right down to the county courthouse and get a license today."

"You're one to talk," Ann grumbled. "You got married in four days' time!"

"Yes, but Callie and I had known each other for a couple months," Rex pointed out. "We'd lived and worked in close proximity to one another. I'm just saying there's no reason to run right out today and get a license. Besides, you don't have time. Because you're going to Oklahoma City to pick up Dad and Meri. Right?"

A lightbulb went on in Ann's brain. "We could get a license in Oklahoma City," she said to Dean, suddenly excited. "Go with me. You're not working right now, and we'll be back tonight. Trust me when I tell you that Dad will be much more supportive than my overprotective big brother."

"Sounds like a plan," Dean agreed, smiling. He glanced at his watch, folding her close as he did so. "Hey, we'd better get going. Donovan will be out of school soon."

They got to their feet in tandem. Rex stood, too, saying, "Look, sis, I just want you to be sure about this."

"I am sure," Ann said stiffly. "I'm sure that

I'm going to marry Dean at the earliest opportunity. I've already got my wedding outfit picked out. All we need now are a pair of gold wedding bands and a license."

"Are you sure that's what you want?" Dean asked softly. "Just simple gold wedding bands?"

She nodded. "Narrow, classic, modest. Everything else is superfluous."

"I sincerely hope you mean that," Rex told her. "However, Dad might be more on my side than you know."

Ann swallowed a sudden lump in her throat, beating back a surge of disappointment. She'd really expected her brother's approval. She hoped he was wrong about their father. Surely she hadn't misunderstood what Dad had meant during their talk at the hospital. On the other hand, her track record with misunderstandings was all too clear. She'd let a simple misunderstanding drive her away from home for years.

Well, she was home now, and Rex would just have to accept that she knew what she was doing. But, oh, she had so hoped that this would be a time of joy for her whole family, especially given her father's illness. At least she knew that Dean's family would take the news well.

Donovan bubbled over with tales of his first day of school. All the way home in the car he rat-

tled on and on about story time and who couldn't
stand in a straight line, write their own names
or recognize certain words. Dean had fretted
about preschool, but when he'd taken Donovan
for evaluation, he'd discovered that his son was
far more advanced academically than most other
children his age, so Dean had made the decision to keep the boy with him rather than pay
for preschool. After all, Donovan got classroom
experience once a week at church. It seemed
he'd done his son no disservice. He judged that
he was about to do both himself and the boy a
great boon, but it troubled Dean that his future
brother-in-law was not more supportive of the
idea.

When they reached the farmhouse, Ann suggested they all sit on the porch. Grandma had
been waiting for their arrival, eager to hear of
Donovan's day, but Dean put her off with a quiet
admonition. "If you don't mind, Ann and I have
an announcement to make."

"The thing is," Ann said to Donovan, reaching up from the rocking chair where she sat to
lace her fingers with Dean's, "I don't want to be
your substitute mom anymore."

Donovan's face fell. Dean almost laughed, but
he patted the boy on the back instead, glanced at
his grandmother, who occupied the other chair,

and quickly said, "What Ann means is that she wants to be your real mom."

Grandma understood at once and clapped her hands together, exclaiming, "Oh, honey!"

"In other words," Ann told Donovan, reaching out to cup Donovan's drooping chin, "your dad and I are going to get married."

Predictably, Donovan's eyes rounded. Then he threw himself into Ann's lap, rocking the chair back on its runners. Laughing, Ann kissed him all over his face. Digger skittered around and wagged his tail enthusiastically.

"We have to go to Oklahoma City to get a marriage license and pick up Ann's father," Dean said, "but we'll be back in time to tuck you into bed tonight."

"Don't go yet," Grandma said, bolting up out of her chair. "Wait right here until I get back." She hurried off at a trot.

"Are you going to have a baby?" Donovan demanded as Grandma disappeared into the house.

Gaping, Ann looked at Dean. "No. Well, not right away. I mean, someday. Don't you want a baby brother or sister?"

"Lots of 'em!" Donovan proclaimed, and both Dean and Ann chuckled.

"We'll take that under advisement," Ann told him, smiling.

"Like father, like son," Dean muttered, squeezing her fingers.

Grandma returned then, something clutched in her hand. "Now, don't feel you have to wear this," she said. "It was Great-Great-Grandma Rosalie's. Milburn bought me one before he knew it existed, and of course I wasn't about to turn it down, so we put this back for our oldest child, except...we didn't trust Wynona not to pawn it, and it's not to Deana's taste. Then we figured it should go to Dean, but if you don't like it, we can always hold it for Donovan." She opened her hand to show them an unusual platinum-and-gold filigreed ring with three round diamonds, two smaller ones on either side of a significantly larger one.

"Oh, my word!" Ann breathed. "That's beautiful!"

"Grandma, I didn't know you had this," Dean said, shocked.

"Honey, don't take this the wrong way," Grandma begged, patting his cheek, "but I didn't want your mother to know about it, and later with things so tight, I—I was afraid you'd want to sell it or use it as collateral."

He hugged her then picked up the ring.

"Ann, what do you think?"

"It's the most unique, meaningful engagement ring I can imagine."

Smiling, he slid it onto her finger, feeling as if his chest might burst. It was a little large, but they could fix that. "We'll take it to a jeweler tomorrow."

"Until then," Ann asked Grandma, "do you have some bandage tape? If I wrap a little piece around the back of the ring, I can wear it now without worrying about losing it."

"I have just the thing," Grandma said.

As she hurried away, Donovan asked Ann, "Will you tuck me in at night?"

"Of course."

"And wash my hair?"

"Naturally."

"Hey, what about me?" Dean teased. He'd been doing these things for years, after all.

Without missing a beat, Donovan said, "She'll tuck you in, too. But you wash your own hair."

Ann bit her lip to keep from laughing, and Dean wondered just how soon they could arrange this small, simple wedding. He hoped Ann was right about her father. If Wes agreed with Rex, she might decide to put things off for a while—and then she might realize what a bad bargain he was.

But no, he wouldn't think like that. Ann agreeing to marry him was an answered prayer. He wouldn't believe anything else.

Grandma seemed to be taking her time finding that tape. He thought he heard the phone ring, so that might explain the delay. She eventually came with it, though, and Ann made the temporary fix. They took their leave, through many hugs and happy farewells.

Back in the car, she looked down at the ring on her finger and sighed.

"I know it's not perfect," he said, "but we'll get it fixed soon."

"It's not that," she assured him. "Really it's not. It's that I love it so much."

He hoped, prayed, that was true, and he kept up that silent prayer all the way to Oklahoma City.

It took longer to get the license than either of them expected, but when Ann called her sister to say they'd been delayed, Meredith told her not to worry. Apparently Wes was doing better than usual. Dean felt some relief that Rex had evidently not called to share their news and argue against their marriage, and he could tell that Ann was also relieved. Nevertheless, as soon as they pushed through the door of the hospital room, Wes barked at both of them.

"It's about time!"

Wes looked wan and weak sitting there in the wheelchair. Strangely, he was dressed in a suit and tie.

"Daddy," Ann said in a confused voice, "why are you dressed like that?"

"It's a surprise!" cried a bright, familiar little voice.

"Donovan!" Dean exclaimed. "Son, what are you doing here?"

"That depends on whether or not you got the license," drawled another familiar voice.

"Rex!" Ann said.

Dean finally looked around. They were all there—almost all—Rex, Meredith, Donovan, Grandma, Wes, everyone but Callie and the baby. As if reading his mind, Rex said, "Callie and Bodie are waiting in the chapel. They wouldn't let the baby up here no matter how much we begged."

"The chapel," Ann repeated. Then she gasped. "I don't believe it!"

"Yes, sister dear, the chapel," Rex said, looking very pleased with himself. "You didn't really believe all that big brother guff back at the ranch, did you?"

"You rat!" Ann scolded, but she was laughing. Then she sobered. "My things."

"Not to worry," Rex told her. "Callie packed you a bag before we left. You have everything you need." He looked to Dean then, adding "Your grandmother packed for you, but I tossed in a few pieces. I have a fairly extensive ward robe that's now too large for me. The shirts and jackets ought to work well enough for you."

"I'm not sure I understand," Dean said, his brow furrowed.

"We're 'loping!" Donovan exclaimed, hopping up and down.

"We drove up with Callie and Bodie," Betty explained, grinning ear to ear.

"I came on my own to get Dad and Meri back home," Rex said. "Now, about that license…"

"The marriage license?" Dean asked, looking at Ann, who burst out laughing.

"That would be the one," Rex chortled. "Did you get it or not?"

"Yeah, we got it," Dean confirmed, still not quite with the program.

"Okay, then," Rex said. "You'll have to change in the men's room downstairs. Annie, you can use this room. When you're ready, Meri will show you where the chapel is."

Dean looked at Ann, who finally confirmed it all for him. "They're throwing us a wedding, darling."

"We're not about to let her kick you to the curb," Rex said happily. "Brothers-in-law with working combines and hay-balers don't come along every day."

Ann put her head back and laughed at that. Wes dug into his coat pocket, producing a small, velvet-covered box. "Here. You're going to need these. My gift to the two of you."

Dean just stood there, so dumbfounded that Ann had to prompt him to take the box. He popped open the hinged lid. Two narrow gold bands nestled inside.

"Perfect," Ann pronounced, a catch in her throat. "It'll go well with my engagement ring." She took a moment to show that off, Callie and Meredith oohing and aahing appropriately while Dean wrapped his mind around the fact that he was about to get married. Married!

"And this is my gift," Meredith said, bringing out a bouquet of mixed white flowers tied with gold ribbon.

"They're exactly right," Ann said, hugging her sister, tears in her eyes.

"My gift," Rex announced, "mine and Callie's, is a suite at the Luxury Hotel here in the city through Friday evening."

"Convenient," Ann said, grinning. "That's an LHI hotel. I'll be able to tender my resignation right after we check in."

"Let's move, people," Wes ordered in a husky voice, "before my meds wear off. That chaplain's not going to wait forever."

"Believe it or not, he said he's done this kind of thing before," Meredith told them.

"Donovan, come with Grandpa." Wes beck

oned. Beaming, Donovan ran to clasp onto Wes's chair. Dean saw that his son wore his best dress pants and a white shirt. A necktie had been tucked into his back pocket.

Married! He was about to get married! And have Ann all to himself until Saturday morning.

Laughing, Dean caught the suitcase Rex shoved at him.

Dean shook his head and winked at Ann, smiling. "Just so you know, I love you enough to completely overlook your crazy family." She laughed, beaming. "And just so *you* know," he said to the grinning about-to-be brother-in-law at his side, "harvesting and hay-baling don't come free. I'm running a business here, and I have a growing family to support."

Rex laughed, shoving him through the door. "We'll negotiate."

"We will," Dean allowed. "And family does get discounts."

What, after all, was business between brothers?

Especially to a man whose every dream had been fulfilled and every prayer answered?

Epilogue

It was a wedding like no other Wes had ever attended. The tiny chapel with its backlit stained glass and few pews contained no altar or dais, only a simple cross upon the wall. No music played. No guests other than the immediate family attended. Then again, his daughter made a bride like no other.

Dressed in shiny gold and white, she looked like a million bucks. Meredith acted as bridesmaid. Rex pushed Wes in his chair at Ann's side, then moved to stand next to Dean and Donovan, who held the rings and could barely contain his excitement. Dean wore almost exactly what Rex had worn for his wedding, dark jeans, black boots, white shirt, black jacket and a string tie. He looked more prone to tears than the bride.

The chaplain kept it simple, leading them both through their vows. Within very few minutes they were at the point of pronouncement, when Dean suddenly lifted a hand as if to bring a halt to the whole proceeding.

"Oh, my word, Jolly!" he said, clapping his hand to his face, the newly installed gold ring on his fourth finger gleaming in the canned light. "I just realized. Sweetheart, you weren't being stupid. You did just what you were supposed to. Think about it. You are a beautiful, talented, intelligent, loving woman. It was a plan to keep some guy from snapping you up while God worked on me. He put you in a safe place and kept you there until the time was right. Until now. For me. For us."

Wes had no idea what that was all about, but Ann certainly did. Lifting her hands to Dean's shoulders, she sniffed back tears and tremulously said, "That's the most beautiful thing I've ever heard."

"What a gift!" Dean exclaimed, pulling her close, his big hands at her trim waist. "I'll never deserve it, but I'll always be thankful for it, and I'll love you until my dying breath."

If Wes had had any doubts about this marriage, they would have vanished on the spot.

Ann wrapped her arms around Dean's neck and went up on tiptoe to kiss him.

The chaplain chuckled and said, "A little premature, but appropriate. I now pronounce you husband and wife."

Everyone applauded and wiped at their tears. Wes gulped down the nausea rising within him and tried not to shiver. Meredith noticed, however, and hurried to hand Ann her bouquet and come for him, picking up a blanket from the front pew as she did so. A blanket in the middle of August. Wes wanted to rage as Meri draped it about his shoulders, but then Donovan grinned at him and waved, posing with his parents as cell phone photos were snapped, and the rage dissipated beneath the weight of his blessings.

Not long ago Wes had feared that he might not live long enough to be a grandpa; now he had two grandchildren, and two of his children had come home to stay. God was good.

For a while now, Wes had wondered why he labored so at Straight Arrow Ranch. For what? For whom? With Gloria gone and his children uninterested in the family concern, the years had begun to seem pointless, but even if God chose not to heal him from this cancer, Wes would forever be thankful that he had lived long enough to see the plan that God had set into motion for his family.

Was it selfish and foolish of him to hope that his youngest child, the one with whom he had the least in common, might also find her way home to stay? She deserved to have more in her life than a spoiled cat.

He told himself that he would be thankful for the time that he and Meredith had together. He would be thankful, but he would also pray. It was a father's privilege and responsibility to pray for his child.

And prayer, as he knew well, availed a man much.

So very much.

* * * * *

*If you loved this story,
check out the first book from
author Arlene James's miniseries*
THE PRODIGAL RANCH

THE RANCHER'S HOMECOMING

*Or pick up these other stories of small-town life
from the author's previous miniseries*
CHATAM HOUSE

*THE DOCTOR'S PERFECT MATCH
THE BACHELOR MEETS HIS MATCH
HIS IDEAL MATCH
BUILDING A PERFECT MATCH*

Available now from Love Inspired!

*Find more great reads at
www.LoveInspired.com*

Dear Reader,

Misunderstandings fuel many of life's problems and decisions. A lack of solid information can have devastating effects on our beliefs, attitudes and actions. Yet, God can use even that to our benefit—and His—when we are surrendered to Him.

Saul misunderstood Who Christ is and the very nature of Christianity. As a result, Saul made some bad decisions and serious mistakes. After he met Jesus on the road to Damascus and learned the full truth, God changed him into Paul and used his past mistakes as a powerful witness, taking Christianity to the gentile world. What a blessing!

We make mistakes. We misunderstand at times and let that color our thoughts and actions. But take heart. Ann and Dean's story illustrates that, when we belong to Him, God is always at work in our lives. He can turn misunderstandings and mistakes into blessings!

God bless you!

Arlene James

LARGER-PRINT BOOKS!

GET 2 FREE
LARGER-PRINT NOVELS
PLUS 2 FREE
MYSTERY GIFTS

Love Inspired®
SUSPENSE
RIVETING INSPIRATIONAL ROMANCE

Larger-print novels are now available...

YES! Please send me 2 FREE LARGER-PRINT Love Inspired® Suspense novels and my 2 FREE mystery gifts (gifts are worth about $10). After receiving them, if I don't wish to receive any more books, I can return the shipping statement marked "cancel." If I don't cancel, I will receive 4 brand-new novels every month and be billed just $5.49 per book in the U.S. or $5.99 per book in Canada. That's a savings of at least 19% off the cover price. It's quite a bargain! Shipping and handling is just 50¢ per book in the U.S. and 75¢ per book in Canada.* I understand that accepting the 2 free books and gifts places me under no obligation to buy anything. I can always return a shipment and cancel at any time. Even if I never buy another book, the two free books and gifts are mine to keep forever.

110/310 IDN GH6P

Name _____ (PLEASE PRINT)

Address _____ Apt. #

City _____ State/Prov. _____ Zip/Postal Code

Signature (if under 18, a parent or guardian must sign)

Mail to the **Reader Service:**
IN U.S.A.: P.O. Box 1867, Buffalo, NY 14240-1867
IN CANADA: P.O. Box 609, Fort Erie, Ontario L2A 5X3

Are you a current subscriber to Love Inspired® Suspense books and want to receive the larger-print edition?
Call 1-800-873-8635 or visit www.ReaderService.com.

* Terms and prices subject to change without notice. Prices do not include applicable taxes. Sales tax applicable in N.Y. Canadian residents will be charged applicable taxes. Offer not valid in Quebec. This offer is limited to one order per household. Not valid for current subscribers to Love Inspired Suspense larger-print books. All orders subject to credit approval. Credit or debit balances in a customer's account(s) may be offset by any other outstanding balance owed by or to the customer. Please allow 4 to 6 weeks for delivery. Offer available while quantities last.

Your Privacy—The Reader Service is committed to protecting your privacy. Our Privacy Policy is available online at www.ReaderService.com or upon request from the Reader Service.

We make a portion of our mailing list available to reputable third parties that offer products we believe may interest you. If you prefer that we not exchange your name with third parties, or if you wish to clarify or modify your communication preferences, please visit us at www.ReaderService.com/consumerchoice or write to us at Reader Service Preference Service, P.O. Box 9062, Buffalo, NY 14240-9062. Include your complete name and address.

LISLP15

WESTERN **WP** PROMISES

YES! Please send me **The Western Promises Collection** in Larger Print. This collection begins with 3 FREE books and 2 FREE gifts (gifts valued at approx. $14.00 retail) in the first shipment, along with the other first 4 books from the collection! If I do not cancel, I will receive 8 monthly shipments until I have the entire 51-book Western Promises collection. I will receive 2 or 3 FREE books in each shipment and I will pay just $4.99 US/ $5.89 CDN for each of the other four books in each shipment, plus $2.99 for shipping and handling per shipment. *If I decide to keep the entire collection, I'll have paid for only 32 books, because 19 books are FREE! I understand that accepting the 3 free books and gifts places me under no obligation to buy anything. I can always return a shipment and cancel at any time. My free books and gifts are mine to keep no matter what I decide.

272 HCN 3070 472 HCN 3070

Name	(PLEASE PRINT)	
Address		Apt. #
City	State/Prov.	Zip/Postal Code

Signature (if under 18, a parent or guardian must sign)

Mail to the **Reader Service:**

IN U.S.A.: P.O. Box 1867, Buffalo, NY 14240-1867
IN CANADA: P.O. Box 609, Fort Erie, Ontario L2A 5X3

WPBPA16R